Bodies, Brews, and Beaches

NOLA ROBERTSON

ISBN: 978-1-953213-35-8

Also by Nola Robertson

A Cumberpatch Cove Mystery

Hawkins Harbor Cozy Mystery

CHAPTER ONE

There it was again. A slow movement. The comforter near my feet shifted slightly from the weight pressing down on the fabric. The sunlight peeking through the blinds of the bedroom window was barely bright enough to see clearly. I didn't need to look at the digital clock sitting on the nightstand to know I'd woken early.

I pretended I was asleep to see what my uninvited stalker would do next. Two more paw steps, and my aunt's cat reached my knees. Luna had upped her stealth tactics. She usually found a place to hide, waiting for the optimal moment to attack.

I opened my eyes in time to see the cat lifting a paw to place on my chest. The Persian had long, soft white fur and a brown mask around her blue eyes. I knew from experience that beneath her gorgeous appearance was a devious creature not to be trifled with. Even so, I couldn't resist cooing, "Good morning, Luna."

Unhappy that she'd been caught, she meowed and jumped to the floor. Instead of heading for the partially open door, she ducked underneath the bed. I didn't mind that Luna was temperamental. It was her feline skills that I had a problem with. She liked to jump up and open my bedroom door, so she could invade my privacy whenever she wanted. Getting up soon and keeping my ankles unscathed meant putting on the pair of socks I kept on the nearby nightstand.

Up until now, Harley, the adorable Havanese I'd adopted, slept peacefully beside me, unaware of his rival's attack. Awakened by the sound of my voice, he sprang to life. He'd missed Luna's retreat, so nuzzling and plying my face with doggy kisses became his priority.

"Hey there, boy." I scratched behind his ears, trying to dodge his tongue. Most of his fur was a reddish brown. The patches of white around his muzzle also covered his chest and ran along his front legs.

My first encounter with the stray pup had included finding a stolen stash of valuables from a local resident. The discovery soon evolved into a sleuthing adventure with my aunt and her friends, Myrna and Vincent. One that ended with solving a string of robberies and a year-old murder.

It hadn't taken long for me to become attached to the little critter and reach a point where finding him a new home hadn't been an option. Even though Archer, my new boss, thought Harley had been abandoned, I didn't want to keep the dog without performing some due diligence first. I searched for Harley's owner by putting an ad in the lost and found section of the local newspaper.

I didn't like focusing on the bad in people, but I wasn't naive enough to believe faults didn't exist. I also wanted to ensure the dog was returning to a good home. To prevent anyone from trying to obtain an animal that didn't belong to them, I'd included the words "proof of ownership required" in the ad. I was greatly relieved when the ad ended, and I hadn't received a single inquiry.

I sat up and threw back the covers. "I think we should get up, don't you?" I asked Harley as I slipped on the socks. He pranced in place, his tail swishing rapidly.

The bed's height made it easily accessible for a dog of

Harley's size. Most days, I could evade the little white paw that shot out from under the bed. Too bad the instant Luna took her first swipe, Harley would know she was in the room, and instead of a regular jump, he'd launch himself off the bed so he could play with her. Playing that generally turned into chasing.

After placing Harley on the floor and watching the animals race from the room, I went about the task of getting ready for work.

As I headed down the stairs to the kitchen where I knew I'd find my aunt, I contemplated the whirlwind changes that had redirected the course of my future. Not only was I Hawkins Harbor's newest resident, but I'd also become the manager of The Flavored Bean, a beach-side coffee shop. The decision I'd made was filled with fresh starts, hope, and absolutely no regrets.

What started as a much-needed vacation with the intent of sorting out my messy life had ended with me falling in love with the area. I decided to choose my own future rather than accept the one that had been selected for me based on the whims of others. More specifically, Stacy Adler, the CEO's daughter from my previous place of employment. I'd been training for several years to take over for my manager when he retired.

I couldn't figure out where Stacy had come up with the idea, but she'd assumed I was a threat to their relationship because I'd dated Rick, her current boyfriend, long before they'd ever met. Rick and I had only gone out a few times, and it was more as friends than anything else. We worked in separate departments on different floors and rarely ran into each other.

Several weeks before my old boss was scheduled to retire, I was notified of my upcoming promotion. Only the company wanted me to relocate to their Minneapolis branch.

I was born in Florida, used to sunshine, plenty of warm weather, and wearing shorts on my days off. Frigid temperatures and shoveling snow were not things I ever wanted to deal with.

My mother, Delia's sister, had been disappointed when I'd told her I'd refused to accept the terms of the promotion. She thought I should've taken the job no matter where I ended up. My father had been neutral on the subject. Aunt Delia was the only one in my family to offer me support, which included an invitation to stay with her as long as I liked.

As much as I enjoyed spending time with my aunt, I couldn't live with her indefinitely. The back of Delia's property faced the beach with a great view of the ocean and was only a few blocks away from the Pelican Promenade Retirement Community, commonly referred to as the Promenade. Unfortunately, Harley had to be kept on a leash whenever he needed to do his business.

Also troubling was Luna's need to constantly torment my dog. Most of the time, I could deal with their playful antics. Delia didn't seem bothered by the barking and chasing that usually ended with her cat perched up high on a shelf in the living room. My aunt's house was beautiful and roomy, but she had a lot of nice belongings, and I worried that it wouldn't be long before something ended up broken.

Now that I felt like I had my job under control, I planned to start looking for a place of my own. Preferably, a house with a fenced-in yard so Harley would have a place to run and play.

Delia was also an early riser and was already dressed and prepared for the day. She might be in her early fifties and retired, but she took care of herself, which showed in her appearance. Her hair was darker than mine and sprinkled with silver, but with similar rounded cheeks and a pert nose, there was no mistaking our familial ties.

Harley was busily finishing whatever my aunt had placed in his food bowl. "Hey," I said as I entered the kitchen.

"Good morning," she said, smiling as she pulled me into a motherly hug. "Are you ready for your first solo day?"

Having breakfast with Myrna and Vincent was part of Delia's daily routine, so she didn't bother making coffee or preparing a meal. Not that I blamed her; the coffee shop had better brews that came in various types and flavors, along with an assortment of freshly baked breakfast items.

Archer was the best kind of boss, one that didn't hover or try to micromanage his employees. He'd wanted someone to take over so he could semi-retire and spend most of his time fishing on his boat.

Having Archer announce that he was leaving in less than twenty-four hours to spend a week fishing on the ocean left me a little stressed. It wasn't because I didn't think I could handle the job. It was because I didn't want to let him down.

"I think so." I smoothed the front of my shirt and shorts that hit mid-thigh. Not having to dress in professional attire was the perk I enjoyed the most.

"I have no doubt, but good luck, anyway," Delia said. "Harley and I will be along shortly."

CHAPTER TWO

I stepped outside and was welcomed by a balmy day. Coastal storms could be brutal, the rainfall heavy and relentless for hours. The one Hawkins Harbor experienced the night before had been the worst I'd seen in a long time. Even though the sun hadn't been shining long when I began my trek from my aunt's house to work, the air was warm and humid. The tawny strands surrounding my face, too short to be pulled back into a ponytail, had already started to curl.

Pools of water covered the uneven surfaces on the neighborhood streets. Broken palm tree branches littered the nearby beach. Areas of the usually debris-free sidewalk had been washed over with sand.

Like every morning since I'd arrived, my daily routine included stopping near the beach and staring out at the ocean. I inhaled a breath of the briny air and, not for the first time, thought about sending Stacy a thank-you basket. Maybe even text her a selfie of me with the beautiful landscape in the background. If not for her unwanted interference in my life, I wouldn't have visited Delia or decided on a new path for my future.

Stacy was too self-absorbed to grasp the irony, so either

of those things would've been a waste of my time. And, there was always a possibility she'd be motivated to find other ways to torment me. Since I preferred having her permanently out of my life, I grinned and continued walking.

The town's main street appeared on my left. The road had been cordoned off from the beach by four-foot-high cylinder posts spaced several feet apart and painted a bright blue. From where I was standing, I could easily see the signs for several clothes boutiques and a souvenir store.

There was a sign posted nearby that read, "Pedestrian Traffic Only. No Vehicles Allowed." Between the visiting tourists and local residents, the shops did a lot of business. I thought the no-traffic idea was a good one, especially for anyone who had rambunctious children who liked to wander off.

I walked a little further and spotted the mint green building that housed my new place of employment. The coffee shop's name was painted on a large wooden sign hanging over the entrance.

Small town businesses had no qualms about using exotic or intriguing methods to attract customers. Painting the outside of their building in pastel or bright colors so they'd be more noticeable was at the top of the list. Not that the stand-alone coffee bar, which also happened to be a renovated house, needed any additional features to be noticed.

It had a raised deck with round, umbrella-covered tables that faced the beach. If the shingled roof had been thatched, the place could've easily been mistaken for a tiki bar. With the palm trees and beach nearby, the area reminded me of something found on a tropical vacation, which was one of the reasons I looked forward to working there.

The place wasn't open for business yet, so I headed to the rear of the building and entered through the back door, locking it behind me. "Good morning, Zoey," I called to Archer's only other employee.

It was no surprise that my stomach rumbled as soon as I inhaled the combined aroma of freshly brewed coffee, baked muffins, and scones filling the air.

"Morning," she called back. "I'm out front."

I found Zoey standing behind the main serving counter, stocking Styrofoam cups. Her crimson curls were pulled back in a ponytail.

She'd worked at the Bean a lot longer than I had and did a great job preparing baked goods and serving beverages. Her lack of interest in being in charge of the place had provided the opening Archer had happily let me fill.

My expertise was in marketing, not the food industry. I had excellent managing skills before Archer offered me the job. I didn't, however, know anything about running the machines responsible for making the various kinds of coffees and drinks listed on the menu. I had no idea if he'd hired me for the position because of his friendship with my aunt, if he'd been impressed with my abilities and thought they'd be useful, or if I'd been his only applicant.

Not that it mattered, because I enjoyed my new job. It might not be the position I'd spent months training for, but at least I didn't have to relocate to Minnesota. And I got to be close to my favorite family member.

Zoey was a pro, and I'd spent the last couple of weeks learning everything I could from her. Even if she hadn't complimented my progress, I'd have to admit I'd done reasonably well at getting the hang of things. Next week, she planned to teach me the food prep side of things. I wasn't bad in the kitchen, but watching her bake was almost magical.

"Is there anything new I should know about?" I asked, more out of habit than anything else. I'd expected the answer to be "no" since we'd spoken late in the afternoon the day before.

Zoey shrugged. "I found a floater."

A floater in Florida could mean any number of things. At first, I thought she'd meant that the coast guard had finally recovered the body of Myles Mumford. His boat was discovered floating in the bay with no one on board. According to the article I'd read, local law enforcement thought he'd fallen overboard, so his death had been reported as accidental. "Where was he found?" I asked, hoping she didn't say on the beach close to our shop.

"In there." She lifted her head and pointed at the fifty-gallon aquarium filling a space in the wall behind the counter.

"Oh." So not a dead body. I leaned closer to get a better look at the miniature corpse bobbing on top of the water. "Is that Herman?"

Zoey liked to assign names to all the non-human life forms she encountered, which included neighborhood strays and the fish in the tank. I didn't want to hurt her feelings by forgetting who was who, but most days, I struggled with learning their names. I only remembered Herman because he was a vibrant blue and stood out from the rest of the fish.

"I'm afraid so," she sounded as if she'd lost someone close to her.

"Um, Zoey," I said, glancing at her over my shoulder. "We can't leave him like that. Why didn't you fish him out?" The aquarium drew a lot of attention. I could only imagine how our customers would feel after seeing a miniature carcass bouncing along on the bubbles from the tank's air filtration system.

"Oh, no, no, no." She held up her hands and slid off her stool. "Archer always took care of dead body disposal."

"We're still talking about the fish, right?" I teased.

"Yes," she giggled, then walked behind the serving counter, grabbed a cup, and scribbled something on the side with a marker.

"Since he's not here and you're in charge, you get to handle it." Zoey held out the cup with Herman's name scrawled on the side and a matching lid. "Please," she added.

It was hard to refuse her request when she added a pout and used a pleading tone. "Fine," I said, snatching the cup out of her hand. "Just so you know, this is my first corpse extraction, so things could get messy." I opened the cabinet beneath the aquarium and retrieved the fish net stashed amongst the rest of the aquatic supplies. "And no laughing." I tried to keep a straight face as I wiggled the net at her.

"Are snide comments allowed?" Zoey asked, chuckling.

I rolled my eyes and lifted the lid on the tank, annoyed by how much she was enjoying my discomfort.

She walked around the counter, then returned a few seconds later with a roll of paper towels.

Scooping Herman out of the water went smoother than getting him out of the net and into the cup without touching his stiff body. "Can you handle things while I take care of you know who?" I asked as I secured the cover on the cup, ensuring that Herman didn't escape from his portable casket during transportation.

"What are you going to do with him?" she asked.

I had several less-than-desirable ideas, but Zoey might not agree with any of them. She was even more soft-hearted about animals than I was.

"Do you really want to know?"

She pursed her lips, then flicked her wrist, signaling me to handle the remains however I wanted.

CHAPTER THREE

My childhood years didn't include taking care of pets, even the kind that stared at you from inside a glass container filled with water. I'd never been privy to any type of disposal process either. Growing up, I'd heard some of the kids in school say their parents had flushed a fish or two down the toilet.

I wasn't a plumbing expert and didn't know if toilet disposal was a good idea. I already had images of Herman bobbing belly up in the aquarium. I didn't need memories of him swirling around the bowl before heading to his final resting place somewhere in the sewer. Once I carried his miniature casket outside, I realized my options weren't much better. I could either bury him somewhere in the decorative plant beds running along the side and front of the building or deposit the cup in the dumpster.

I was afraid that a neighborhood cat might be inclined to dig up the poor fish's body and make a snack out of it. "Sorry, bud," I said to the cup. "I'm afraid a shallow grave is out, so it will have to be the dumpster."

The stench of rotting garbage clung to the air in the area around the large blue container and got considerably worse the moment I got closer. I started to doubt my decision about finding a shovel and digging a hole. I might have changed my mind about the dumpster if I hadn't gotten caught lifting the lid.

"Brinley," Delia said as she strolled around the corner of the building with Myrna and Harley walking beside her.

Startled, I squeaked and released the lid, the metal making a loud clank when it hit the rim. "Hey, guys," I said, taking several deep breaths, hoping my heated cheeks weren't blazing a bright red.

"Sorry, we didn't mean to scare you," Myrna said.

She had a stocky build and couldn't be more than three inches over five feet, yet she'd managed to wrap her arms around my neck, then squeeze as if it had been months instead of a single day since she'd seen me last. The first time I'd met her, Vincent had warned me she was a hugger, something she'd proven every day since then.

Her curly strands had more silver than dark brown. Judging by her bright yellow tennis shoes and purple socks, which didn't match the rest of her outfit, I got the impression she didn't care about fashion trends.

"We got here a little early," Delia said.

"When we saw you walk behind the building, we thought we'd say hello while we waited for you and Zoey to open," Myrna added.

"Hey, boy," I said, reaching down to scratch Harley's head. He was on his leash and happily prancing next to my aunt. Seeing his tail swish faster when he saw me always warmed my heart.

Delia glanced around curiously, then said, "I could've sworn I heard you talking to someone."

"Yeah," I said, a little embarrassed that I'd been caught before I could toss the cup in the garbage. "We had an unfortunate departure, and I got elected for disposal duty." I held up the container so they could see the name Zoey had written on the side. "I figured the dumpster would be the best and safest place to leave him, given the cat activity in the area."

"Oh," Delia said. "You're probably right."

I was relieved when neither of them disapproved of my disposal choice. Harley nudged my leg with his snout, so I gave his head another scratch before walking over to the dumpster and lifting the lid.

"Wait," Myrna said, waving her hands. "You can't toss him in without saying a few words first." She sniffed and dabbed beneath her eye. "Herman brought a lot of joy to so many customers."

I'd also enjoyed watching the fish swim around the aquarium, but not enough to lose tears over his departure. At this rate, I'd never be able to get rid of the cup and wondered how long it would take before Zoey started to worry or came out to look for me.

I had no clue what memorable words should be spoken and held the cup out to Myrna. "Maybe you should do the honors since you've known him longer than I have."

Myrna stared at the cup and rubbed her chin. "You were a big fish among water dwellers, and we will never forget you." She tossed the cup in the bin and smiled. "Now, how about breakfast?"

Caught off guard by Myrna's change in behavior, I flashed Delia an inquiring look, which earned me a shrug.

"Zoey should have the place open by now, so why don't you two go inside," Delia said. "I'll catch up with you after I take Harley for a quick walk on the beach."

My dog was faster at doing his business when he didn't have someone following him around. "Do you need one of these?" I asked, reaching into the pocket of my shorts and pulling out the plastic bag I kept for any presents he left on the ground.

"Keep it. I have plenty," Delia said, patting the travel pack she had attached to her hip.

The orange-striped tabby cat Harley had chased the day I'd found him picked that moment to emerge from behind a nearby palm tree. Not long after our first sighting of the cat, Zoey had named the animal Quincy. We couldn't get close enough to tell if it was a male or female, but she was convinced the name fit either gender.

"No. Don't," I said, too late to stop Delia from unclipping Harley's leash from his collar. As soon as he barked and took off running, the cat ducked between some trees. I knew from their last encounter that Harley wouldn't hurt the feline, that announcing his presence and chasing were part of his territorial display.

Harley was good about not straying far, and I'd expected him to stop once he reached the nearest palm tree. Instead, he kept running and disappeared from sight.

"Darn it, Harley. Get back here," I called and started after him.

The previous night's storm had left some soggy spots in the sand, and my shoes sunk with every step I took. It would've been more fun if I'd been strolling along the beach barefoot.

Harley's barking had changed, the tone laced with agitation. Gripped by an uneasiness I couldn't explain, I hurried to reach the area past the trees covered with boulders, shrubbery, and tall grass.

The cat was nowhere in sight, but Harley had stopped and was frantically pawing the dirt, a flurry of sand and dirt spraying the air behind him. I'd been so worried about catching him that I hadn't gotten his leash from Delia first.

"Hey, boy," I said, slowly creeping toward him, so I could grab his collar and keep him from taking off again. Not that he had any interest in going anywhere. Whatever he'd found had his complete attention because he acted as if he hadn't even noticed me.

He stopped digging and latched onto a piece of fabric. I moved closer and noticed that the cloth wasn't pulling free. "What have you got there?"

Once I realized the material Harley tugged was wrapped around a human arm sticking out of the sand, I was sorry I'd asked. Every time he pulled, a pale, stiff hand slapped against the ground. It took a few seconds more to completely grasp that my dog was growling and pulling on a dead body partially buried in the sand.

I wasn't prone to overreacting, but I'd never had to deal with a lifeless corpse before and was proud of myself for not screaming hysterically like the heroine in a thriller movie.

"Harley, no!" I yelled. "Drop it." I hurried over and snatched him off the ground, glad that the shirt didn't rip in my haste to get him away from the arm.

Bodies didn't bury themselves on the beach, which meant someone had gone to a lot of trouble to hide this one. If the severe storm hadn't washed away some of the sand, there's a good chance the person I was backpedaling away from might not have been found for quite some time. At the moment, I truly wished someone else had made the discovery.

Since the man was positioned on his side, I'd gotten a look at his sand-covered head and a partial glimpse of his face. Thankfully, his eyes were closed, and my memory wouldn't be etched with images of a death stare. His features seemed familiar, though I didn't think he was anyone I'd met since moving to town.

"Oh good, you found him," Myrna said as she and Delia approached from the opposite direction. They'd no doubt planned to intercept Harley if he'd intended to go past the rocks and continue running along the beach.

Delia smiled and patted Harley's head when I walked over to join them.

Myrna studied my face and furrowed her brows. "He didn't get the cat, did he?" She jerked her head back and forth as if searching for a furry carcass.

"No, Quincy got away," I said.

"Brinley, you look pale. Is everything okay?" Delia asked.

From where we were standing, I knew if I stepped out of the way, they'd be able to see the top half of the man's body and the back of his head. "I'm fine. Unfortunately, what Harley found isn't doing well." I jutted my chin over my shoulder toward my dog's discovery. I had to tighten my grip because Harley was whining and squirming. He wanted to get back down, most likely to finish what he'd started.

Delia sidestepped to see around me. Her complexion lightened, no doubt mirroring mine. "Well, that's not good."

"No, it's not," I said, wishing again that my dog didn't have a knack for finding or digging up things that were crime related.

"What's not good?" Myrna asked. Even with glasses, her vision wasn't always the best. She moved to my right, then leaned forward and squinted. "Oh."

Myrna seemed relatively calm under the circumstances. I would've asked how many dead bodies she'd been this close to, but I didn't want to know the answer.

"Why didn't you tell us you were a dead body magnet?" Myrna asked.

"Because I'm not," I said, shooting her a sidelong glance after she'd made it sound like I found a body every other day.

Myrna pushed her glasses farther up her nose. "Are you sure because I don't think finding two corpses on the same day is a coincidence?" She tapped her chin. "More like an omen."

There were days when trying to understand Myrna's logic was a waste of time. I shook my head. Technically, Zoey was the one who'd found Herman. I refrained from pointing out that the fish had died from natural causes and wasn't a full-grown person who'd obviously been murdered. The who and why would have to wait.

"Do you think the dead guy could be a pirate?" Myrna asked, then widened her eyes. "Oh, and if he is, then maybe he buried a treasure somewhere around here. We'll have to ask Vincent if pirates sailed our coastline."

Vincent had been a computer engineer before he

retired. He also enjoyed researching a wide range of topics, sometimes to the point of being an expert. I wouldn't be surprised if he knew all about pirate lore.

"If he was a pirate, I'm pretty sure we'd be looking at a skeleton, not a hand covered with skin," Delia said.

"Well, that's disappointing," Myrna grumbled. "A treasure hunt would've been a lot of fun."

"I agree," I said. "Since searching for gold is out of the question, maybe now would be a good time to call the police." I held Harley out to Delia. "Would you mind?"

"Not at all." She happily took him so I could pull the phone out of my back pocket. I swiped my finger across my contact list, dread sweeping across my skin as I scrolled for Carson's mobile number. I knew the deputy wouldn't be thrilled that this was the second crime I'd been involved with since I'd come to town.

In my defense, I hadn't been a resident long enough for anyone to irritate me to the point of wanting to kill them. Not that being vindictive or malicious was even in my nature. I felt certain I didn't have to worry about being treated as a suspect. At least I hoped not.

"I'll be right back," Myrna said, then sprinted off in the same direction I'd arrived. For an elderly woman, she could move when she wanted to and was gone before I could say anything to her. Maybe it was the sneakers, though I doubted it.

"Where is she going?" I asked Delia.

My aunt rolled her eyes as if it was obvious. "To get Vincent, of course. If we're going to help solve the murder, he'll need to see the body and the crime scene before the police arrive."

Vincent was prompt when it came to appointments and gatherings. He was no doubt waiting for Delia and Myrna at their usual table on the deck outside the Bean, wondering what had happened to them.

I could've gone the rest of the day, maybe even the year, without hearing they planned to get involved...again.

With a frustrated groan, I swiped the screen. Carson answered on the second ring. After the burglary thing, he'd given me his number to use in case of emergencies. After a warm greeting, his voice took on the serious, suspicious tone I'd heard on numerous occasions. "Is something wrong?"

"You could say that," I said, then went on to give him a brief explanation of what Harley had found.

"Don't touch anything," he said.

"No problem." Complying would be easy. I had no intention of getting any closer to the body.

"And make sure no one else does either." There was another pause as if he was trying to decide what other directives he should give me. "I'll be there shortly."

I'd barely disconnected the call and tucked the phone in my back pocket again when Myrna returned with Vincent. He was quite a bit taller than her and had thin wisps of hair covering a balding head. If I didn't know he was a local, the navy blue fanny pack clipped around his waist, along with the red floral shirt and khaki shorts, would've made me think he was a tourist.

"Can you tell how long the body's been here?" Myrna asked him as soon as they reached Delia and me.

Vincent rarely smiled. He wrinkled his nose, his frown deepening. "I'm not an expert on dead things," he said. "I have no idea how long this one's been here."

"Maybe we can tell how long he's been in the ground if we pinch the flesh and see if it's still squishy," Myrna said, taking a step in the direction of the body.

I wasn't normally squeamish, but visualizing what she planned to do made my empty stomach churn, and I was glad I hadn't eaten anything yet. I touched her arm to stop her. "No," I said. "You can't. Carson didn't sound happy that Harley and I already disturbing things."

"It's too bad Harley didn't uncover more of the body so we could see if there are any injuries," Vincent said. "Maybe discern the cause of death."

Sometimes the man's analytical side bordered on morbid. He might be okay with seeing the damage done to the corpse, but I wasn't. It was bad enough that I'd have nightmares about the flopping hand for a long time.

"How does Carson expect us to figure out who the dead guy is if he won't let us get close enough to see the face?" Myrna asked.

"I'm sure keeping us from interfering was the point," Delia said.

"Or maybe he wanted to make sure we didn't disturb any clues," I said, feeling a little guilty that Harley and I had made Carson's job more difficult.

"Doesn't matter," Vincent said as he unzipped his pack and pulled out binoculars a little larger than glasses used at an opera.

"Why are you carrying those around?" Delia asked before I could.

"Bird watching, mostly," Vincent said, holding them in front of his eyes. "But they have other uses."

It was the 'other uses' that worried me. I thought about closing my eyes and covering my ears. If Vincent got caught using the binoculars for something a little less legal, then I couldn't be called as a witness.

"Come on, we'll move to the other side," Vincent said, motioning us to follow him. "I promise we won't mess with Carson's crime scene."

Was it wrong that I was the only one reluctant to follow him?

Vincent had us gather in a spot that gave us a blurry yet direct line of sight to the body. So far, we'd gotten lucky that neither of the pedestrians strolling along the sidewalk had bothered to notice us. After glancing around one more time to make sure no one else saw what he was doing, Vincent held the binoculars up to his eyes and fiddled with the adjustment. "I can't be totally sure, but I think the body belongs to Myles Mumford."

"No way," Myrna said. "He's supposed to be floating

somewhere in the ocean, being fish food, or possibly feeding sharks."

"Myrna," I said, my tone chastising.

Vincent returned the binoculars to his pack. "If I'm right, and that is him, then the bigger question would be how he got there and who was responsible?"

"It sounds like *someone* needs to find out who did this, and soon," Delia clipped the leash to Harley's collar and handed him back to me. "I don't think a dead body on the beach will be good for business."

I set my dog on the ground, hoping the 'someone' she was referring to wasn't the three people standing next to me.

CHAPTER FOUR

Myrna told me that Zoey was opening up the Bean for business when she'd gone to retrieve Vincent, so she'd told her about our discovery. Not that I thought for a second that Myrna would be able to keep the information to herself.

I figured Carson would have questions when he arrived and wouldn't want to ask them in front of a bunch of people. Mornings were our busiest time of the day, and I hated leaving Zoey all by herself. I sent her a text letting her know I'd be in to help after I talked to the police.

No one walking near the beach could see the body without traipsing past the palm trees and boulders, so I urged Myrna, Vincent, and Delia to wait with me on the sidewalk. Harley was back on his leash, pacing and sniffing the ground, no doubt looking for something else to investigate. Thankfully, the cat hadn't reappeared, which kept my dog from barking and drawing attention to us.

Pedestrian traffic was picking up. Some of the people were customers and offered a friendly greeting as they walked past us. So far, no one asked why I was standing outside instead of being inside working behind the counter. Maybe because they knew Delia was my aunt and assumed we were having a family-related conversation.

The people in small towns always seemed to have a natural ability to sense when something mysterious had taken place. It wouldn't take long before word spread about what we'd found once Carson arrived.

Since vehicles weren't allowed to access the main street, the town had built a large parking lot to accommodate visitors and anyone who wanted to visit the beach. When Carson said he'd be arriving shortly, he hadn't been kidding. A member of law enforcement running would've drawn too much attention, so he'd approached us at a steady but moderate pace. Being tall with long legs helped him cover the distance faster.

"That was quick," I said by way of a greeting.

"I was already on my way to the Bean for coffee," he said.

He was dressed in his uniform and most likely on his way to work when I'd called him. Carson wasn't a regular customer like my aunt and her friends, but he did stop by a couple of times during the week.

"Are you okay?" he asked.

"Yeah," I said. I didn't think I'd sounded like I was on the verge of hysterics when I'd called him. Maybe I was wrong. Perhaps he was being thoughtful, or maybe he'd been trained to offer support to people who'd discovered a body.

As far as I knew, Hawkins Harbor didn't have a high body count unless someone considered the elderly who died of natural causes. Something that couldn't be avoided with a retirement neighborhood in the community.

"Why don't you show me what you found," Carson said. "Just Brinley." He held up his hand when Delia, Myrna, and Vincent started moving.

Myrna snorted and crossed her arms but didn't argue.

I handed the end of Harley's leash to Delia, then led Carson between the palm trees and around the rocks, stopping near the edge of the tall grass and in view of the partially exposed body. "Over there," I said, pointing.

He scanned the area with his dark gaze as if scrutinizing, then noting every detail. "Is this how you found it?" he asked.

"Yeah, kind of," I said. "Harley was digging around the hand, so the paw prints are his." I cringed at the mess my dog had made.

"The footprints are mine. I didn't let anyone else near the body." I ignored the skeptical look he shot me. Checking the ground for prints before and after finding the corpse hadn't been a consideration, so I didn't know if someone had been there before me. If he decided to press the issue, I could easily prove I was telling the truth by showing him the trail in the sand our entourage had made when I'd led them away from the area. "You might find cat prints as well. Harley was chasing the stray that hangs out around here."

"Anything else?" he asked.

"Actually, yes. Harley was tugging on the shirt sleeve so your lab guys will find teeth marks and doggy saliva." After participating in quite a few online mystery game sessions with my aunt and her friends, I'd learned quite a bit about forensics and investigative procedures. I had no idea how accurate the game's details were but assumed they had to be close.

"I'll be sure to let them know." Surprisingly, Carson didn't scoff. He did, however, work hard to suppress a grin.

"Come on," he said. "I'll walk you back."

"Don't you need to take a closer look at the body first?" I was hoping to get confirmation on Vincent's speculation that Myles was the dead guy.

"He's not going anywhere." He held out his arm, motioning me to leave.

Once he'd instructed me to wait with the others, Carson moved out of hearing range to make some calls. Not long after that, another officer I'd never met arrived.

He walked with a confident swagger and had a fresh-out-of-high-school appearance. His light brown hair was cropped short, and he wore a uniform similar to Carson's.

"So, we've got a dead body, huh?" he asked as he strolled over to Carson. He scanned the area, seemingly excited about the prospect of seeing a corpse.

"Yes," Carson said. "I need you to tape off this area of the beach. And once you're done with that, I want you to keep everybody away from the crime scene. No one gets in. Am I clear?"

"Um, yes, sir." The officer fumbled with the keys he'd pulled out of his pocket. "I need to go back to my car and get the tape."

Carson sighed and rubbed his nape. "You do that."

I felt sorry for the officer. Carson could be intimidating when he switched into his law enforcement role. "Who's the new guy?" I asked my aunt. I was good with faces and didn't remember ever seeing him in the Bean.

Delia leaned toward me and whispered, "That's Douglas Dankworth."

"He's new," Vincent muttered. "And only been on the job a couple of months."

"So I gathered," I said.

Myrna touched my arm. "He's a nice guy but not as good-looking as Carson." She shot the deputy an appreciative smile. "Douglas might be a bit young for you. Maybe we should try to match him up with Zoey."

There were several women in the community, including my aunt, Myrna, and their friend Leona, who considered themselves matchmaking professionals. When I'd first visited Hawkins Harbor, I hadn't been in town an entire day before the three women began pointing out the eligible bachelors they thought would interest me.

I understood why Carson had been at the top of their list. He was handsome, personable, and had a good sense of humor when he wasn't scowling and scolding us about not getting involved with police matters. According to the ladies who attended many of the Promenade events, he was also a good dancer.

Unfortunately, I wasn't interested in anything more than being friends and hadn't noticed any indication that he was either.

"I hadn't even thought about that," Delia said.

"And maybe we can save this discussion for another time." I didn't want them concentrating on my love life, but I wasn't willing to let them refocus their efforts on my friend either.

"Brinley's right," Delia said. "We can chat about it later."

"That's not exactly what I meant," I said, though I was sure my aunt hadn't misinterpreted my meaning.

By the time Douglas returned, people were gathering, and it wouldn't take long for Carson to be inundated with questions. I'd been gone longer than expected and was worried about Zoey. People who had to wait longer than normal for their first cup of coffee didn't always remain friendly. I didn't want her subjected to irate customers. "Would it be alright if I head back to the Bean?" I asked Carson.

"I don't see why not," he said. "I'll let you know if I have any more questions." He glanced at Myrna, Vincent, and Delia. "Will I be wasting my breath if I remind the more mature, sophisticated, and should-definitely-know-better people in the group to leave the investigating to the professionals?"

I knew he was referring to the others, but he'd included me when he pinned everyone in the group with his intense glare. Not that I could blame him. I hadn't exactly been a bystander when they'd investigated the neighborhood robberies.

"Absolutely not," Delia said with the calm practiced charm of a professional fabricator.

Carson seemed to have a hard time believing her, but after a few seconds of deliberation, he said, "You three can go as well."

CHAPTER FIVE

As soon as Carson excused himself so he could return to his job, Delia, Myrna, and Vincent headed for their usual table out on the deck. Harley followed along and made himself comfortable near my aunt's feet. They had a good view of the police activities from where they were sitting. I was certain if they gleaned any additional information or learned the dead person's identity, they'd share the details with me later.

I used the door at the back of the building to enter the Bean. The aroma inside teased my senses and reminded me that I'd dealt with two deaths this morning on an empty stomach and without the aid of a caffeine-laden brew. With the place filled with customers, sneaking off to grab a bite and drink some coffee wasn't going to happen anytime soon.

After stopping in the restroom to use the facilities and remove the sandy paw prints Harley left on the front of my shirt, I grabbed an apron from a hook in the prep area and headed up front to help Zoey.

I'd gotten used to the shop being a social hub, but I wasn't prepared for all the customers milling about the place. It appeared Delia was wrong about a death on the beach being bad for business. Everyone who didn't already have a drink or one of our baked goods was standing in line waiting to place an order. I wouldn't want the discovery of a dead body to be part of my everyday routine, but I wasn't going to complain about the shop gaining additional income.

Some of the newcomers were standing in small crowds chatting. Others had their faces pressed near the glass windows that faced the outside deck and the beach beyond. I recognized a handful of people I knew had jobs that started early. Apparently, reports of a newly discovered corpse took precedence over being late for work.

If the dead guy was Myles Mumford, then there was a good chance he was killed by a local. Anyone inside the shop could be a potential killer, which meant I needed to pay attention, and hopefully learn some much-needed clues.

Brady Noonan, one of the few, was standing off to the side, talking with two young women I didn't recognize. Judging by their laughter, the females seemed more interested in his flirting than what was going on outside.

I couldn't blame the women for being interested in Brady. The man had a muscular build, silky blond hair, and an easy-going charm. He owned his own lawn maintenance company and serviced quite a few lawns, including my aunts. His sister Avery, who I had yet to glimpse, was the event coordinator at the Promenade.

In order to reach the area where Zoey was working, I had to walk past the counter with barstools that ran parallel to the wall with the aquarium. Marjorie Cooper, and her son Hugh, who frequently came into the shop, were perched on the last two stools closest to my destination.

Hugh was always friendly during their visits, but Marjorie had a snobbish side and demonstrated her superior attitude most of the time. I'd learned from Delia that they came from money somewhere up north. Marjorie had retired to the area several years ago after her husband died. Hugh traveled quite a bit, so I didn't know if he resided with his mother, had his own place in town, or if he spent a lot of time visiting.

Because of her head of solid silver curls and the additional wrinkles I was convinced she'd derived from frowning, it was hard to determine Marjorie's age. I guessed her to be somewhere in her late sixties or early seventies. After years spent dealing with his mother's difficult personality, I found it interesting that Hugh only had a few gray hairs intermingled with his dark strands.

They each had a coffee and a plate with a partially eaten scone sitting on the counter in front of them. Hugh was about to take another bite when Marjorie said, "I don't care if she's Delia's niece. How do we know Archer didn't hire a serial killer?" She wrinkled her nose. "We didn't have bodies piling up on the beach before she got here."

One dead person didn't qualify as a pile, nor did it mean the town had a serial killer in their midst. I tried not to take the accusation personally. I was the new person in town, so of course, some of the older residents were going to assume I had something to do with the recently deceased.

Hugh patted Marjorie's shoulder. "Now, mother, we've known Archer a long time. He's not the kind of man who goes around hiring killers. I'm sure if Carson thought she was responsible, he wouldn't have let her come back to work."

As soon as Marjorie noticed me, I pretended like I hadn't heard their comments. I put on my best professional smile, then slipped behind the counter and made my way toward them. "Good morning, Marjorie, Hugh."

"Good morning, Brinley," Hugh said.

The man deserved a complimentary breakfast for coming to my rescue, but I was afraid that Marjorie might accuse him of conspiring with me if I didn't charge him. I certainly didn't want to be responsible for making him the target of more unpleasantness.

"I was about to tell Marjorie that you probably don't know who you found on the beach," Hugh said. He must've realized I'd overheard them because he flashed me a discreet wink.

"Is that true?" Marjorie asked, her tone demanding. "You have no idea who it is?"

"I'm afraid not," I said. "I should get back to work." Before Marjorie decided to share her opinions or ask me more body-related questions, I added, "Enjoy your day." I gave them a friendly wave, then headed for the preparation area.

Zoey was great with customers and could handle an influx of people. I was relieved to find her flitting about in her usual calm and upbeat manner. Though leaving her alone hadn't been my fault, I still felt guilty for abandoning her. "Are you doing okay?"

"Fine," she said, pausing long enough to glance over her shoulder. "How about you?" Concern flickered in her green eyes.

I was actually doing fairly well, given the circumstances. "I'm good, but who knew heading up fish disposal would lead to all this?" I teased, hoping to alleviate her worry.

She pulled a lever to fill a cup with coffee. "I assume Herman had a good send-off."

"Yep. Myrna even said a few words for him."

Zoey chuckled and shook her head. "Sounds like something she'd do."

Any other questions would have to wait. I looked at the notepad where she'd jotted down the order she was working on. Using a metal tong, I snagged a blueberry muffin and placed it on a plate. "What else do you need?"

"I can handle this if you want to help the next person in line," Zoey said, continuing to fill the order by placing drinks on a tray.

"Works for me." I walked over to the counter to help the next customer, who happened to be Dean Swafford, the owner of Swafford's Bait and Tackle shop located down by the marina. He wasn't a daily customer, but he did manage to come by a few times a week. Because he and Archer were friends, I'd learned his name and where he worked via an introduction from my boss. "Morning, Dean. What can I get you?"

Typically, he was fairly chatty, but like almost everyone else in the place, he appeared to be preoccupied with what was going on outside. "Um, Dean," I said again when he didn't respond.

"Oh, sorry." His cheeks flushed, and he gave the menu mounted on the wall behind me a quick glance. "I guess I'll have a large coffee…black."

"Are you sure you don't want a scone or muffin to go with that?" I asked.

"No." He paused. "And can you make it to go?"

"Sure."

Once I'd gotten Dean his drink and taken his payment, helping the rest of the people in line went rather quickly.

During that time, almost everyone I spoke to wanted to know the dead guy's identity. Since I didn't know for sure, I wasn't about to fuel any rumors with Vincent's thoughts on the subject. I'd also glimpsed a gurney being wheeled down the sidewalk with a bag containing the victim's body.

Shortly after that, the customers who weren't regulars, and those who didn't usually tend to linger, left. No more corpse meant nothing left to see. The disappointing comments and groans reminded me of how people reacted when they heard the last call for drinks in a bar.

"Why don't you take a break," I said to Zoey. "You've more than earned it."

"Thanks," she said, reaching under the counter for a porcelain cup. After pouring a coffee, she settled on one of the bar stools with her latest romance novel and started reading.

Being the manager came with perks, and I didn't need to stay behind the counter to keep an eye on things. When the place was almost empty, I prepared a tray with a fresh round of drinks for Delia, Myrna, and Vincent. I also added a coffee and a muffin for myself, then headed outside.

"I don't suppose Carson popped over to give you any more details about what happened to you know who, did he?" I asked as I placed their cups on the table and removed the empty ones.

"No," Myrna said, releasing a disappointed sigh. She crossed her arms and slumped back in her chair. "Which seems rude since you found the body for him."

Her response wasn't unexpected. My aunt and her friends might consider themselves mystery sleuthers, but Carson had other ideas. Before I'd ever visited the town, their attempts at investigating had gotten them on the wrong side of the deputy.

"I don't think he'll tell us even if he does know," Vincent said.

"The body was bagged up when they rolled it away, so we couldn't get a better look at who was inside," Delia said.

After giving Harley a few scratches, I turned the chair next to Delia so it was facing the beach before settling into it. As I sipped my coffee, an older man wearing a uniform similar to Carson's strutted toward the crime scene as if his arrival took precedence over any murder. His dark hair was peppered with silver, his shirt straining around his mid-section.

Carson didn't look very happy to see the man. By the way Douglas cringed when he lifted the tape to allow him access to the crime scene; I didn't think he was thrilled either. "Who's that?" I asked.

"Landon Lennox," Myrna said, her voice laced with disdain.

"Our pompous sheriff," Vincent added with a snort.

"Personally, I think Carson should be in charge. From what I've seen, Landon doesn't have a clue how to do real police work."

It was rare for them to dislike someone so vehemently. Delia hadn't said anything, but I got the impression if she did, her comment wouldn't be favorable. I was curious to know what the man had done to gain the low opinion. If the table on the other end of the deck wasn't still occupied and within hearing distance, I would've asked for additional details.

Zoey poked her head outside. "Are you guys still getting together tonight?"

Before I arrived in Hawkins Harbor, Myrna, Vincent, and Delia met at least one night a week in one of their homes to play the online video game "Crimes Galore Murder Mysteries." When Zoey wasn't busy with her social life, she'd popped by and participated.

"Of course," Delia said. "I'll send you a text later to let you know where we're meeting."

"Great. I can't wait," Zoey said, then disappeared inside.

Zoey sounded too enthusiastic about an evening spent gaming, which sent a feeling of dread zipping through my system. I turned to my aunt. "You guys aren't planning on getting involved again, are you?"

"Involved in what?" Myrna asked. Feigning innocence wasn't one of her stronger skills.

I pointed at the beach. "Dead guy. Murder."

"We don't even know who it is for sure," Delia said. Her sweet, placating tone would've been believable if she hadn't played a parental role throughout most of my life.

"Yet," Vincent muttered, earning him narrow-eyed glares from both women.

I didn't need to ask if they were serious about ignoring Carson's warning. The look they shared was confirmation enough. I also knew from their last sleuthing adventure that I wouldn't be able to talk them out of it, which meant they'd need supervision, and I'd be tagging along to keep them out of trouble.

CHAPTER SIX

The Bean closed at two, but it took Zoey and me another hour to finish cleaning up and do some basic prep work for the next day. I was exhausted by the time I reached Delia's house. I was glad to hear that the group had already decided to meet at her place instead of Vincent's or Myrna's. It meant I didn't need to dress for a social visit, and could get away with wearing sweats and a T-shirt.

Though I'd never admit it out loud, I enjoyed going to Vincent's home. He had a huge television screen mounted on the wall that enhanced our mystery-solving gaming experience.

Not that I was hooked on playing the game or anything. If anyone asked, I would proudly boast that I was the newest member of the Hawkins Harbor Super Sleuthers online team; HHSS for short.

Every now and then, Myrna would bring a video game that featured a zombie apocalypse. I had no interest in playing, but watching her and Vincent kill the undead with a vengeance was entertaining. Delia said she didn't care much for slaughtering the online monsters either, but it didn't stop her from occasionally playing the game anyway.

After Myrna and Vincent arrived, we headed for the bedroom Delia had turned into a spacious office. They settled on a cushioned sofa that easily accommodated three people and faced a wall-mounted, flat-screen television. I took my usual spot in a matching chair that sat perpendicular to the right side of the couch.

A desk and computer sat in a corner near the window. The tripod, board, and colored markers Vincent had contributed to our robbery investigation were still sitting on the floor against a wall not far from the screen.

"So," Myrna said, eagerly clapping her hands together. "When you took the training wheels off this morning, I'll bet you didn't expect to end up knee-deep in a murder."

I assumed she was talking about my first day of work without Archer's supervision. "You're right about that," I said, settling back into the comfortable cushions. "This had to be the most dreadful and exciting day I've ever had."

Managing the Bean was the easy part. The shop had even experienced record sales for the month. Too bad it took finding a dead body to gain the additional exposure. It definitely wasn't a marketing technique I'd recommend, nor was it something I never wanted to experience again. Not that the shop didn't regularly already make a good profit. My boss had done an excellent job of building up his business.

"Speaking of going solo, have you heard from Archer since he left?" Delia asked.

"No, but I sent him a text, and I'm sure he'll check in once he gets it," I said.

The body might have been found on a public beach, but it wasn't far from the Bean. I hated interrupting his semi-retirement, but since he was the owner, I thought Archer should know what had happened in his absence.

He'd lived in town his entire life and knew most of the inhabitants. If Myles was the person Harley and I found, there was a good chance Archer knew him. Zoey might know if the two men had a friendly relationship, but until the police released the dead guy's identity to the public, I didn't want to say anything.

I had no idea what kind of cell service he'd get out on the ocean. Unless Archer turned off his phone, I was certain it would start working as soon as he returned to shore. I didn't want to worry the others, but I was also concerned that he might have gotten caught in the storm. The sooner he checked in, the better I'd feel.

The doorbell rang, startling me and causing Harley to jump up from the floor. He ran past Delia to be the first one to the door, barking all the way. Whoever was at the door must have been someone he recognized because his doggy noises didn't last long.

Mumbled voices accompanied the footsteps I heard approaching in the hallway. "Did you guys hear the latest?" Zoey asked as she hurried into the room with Harley prancing closely beside her. She had a plastic bag hooked over her wrist and was carrying a pale pink box with the name "**Tori's Tasty Treasures**" printed on the side in bold purple letters.

"Latest what?" I asked.

"News about the body you found," she said. "They've confirmed that it was Myles Mumford."

When none of us acted surprised, Zoey narrowed her green gaze into an accusing glare. "You already knew." She slumped her shoulders, the notion that she'd been left out of something important obvious on her wounded expression. "Why didn't you tell me?"

"His face was coated with sand, so we couldn't tell for sure," I said.

"We were afraid to say anything in case we were wrong," Delia said. She pushed off the sofa and moved around the coffee table to give Zoey one of her motherly hugs. The same comforting hug she'd given me my entire life when my mother, who believed her way was the only way, refused to provide me with any kind of support.

"You're one of us. We would never intentionally leave you out of the loop."

"Really?" Zoey asked.

"Of course," Myrna said.

I nodded and smiled. Vincent grunted, which for him was a big deal, and made Zoey grin.

"Well, then you should know that people think Myles was involved in some international antique smuggling," Zoey said. "That he double-crossed someone, and they killed him for it."

"No," Myrna gasped.

"I don't think that's possible," Vincent said, rolling his eyes. "He owns a souvenir shop and, as far as I know, he never traveled overseas."

"Where did you hear that?" Delia asked. After reassuring Zoey, she'd slipped from the room and returned, carrying bottled water for each of us.

"When I stopped by Tori's to pick up some cheesecake for us, everyone in the place was talking about him and tossing out random speculations." Zoey placed the box of delectables in the center of the coffee table and out of Harley's reach. Next, she opened the bag and pulled out paper plates, napkins, and plastic forks, arranging them neatly next to the box.

"Sorry, boy, but these aren't for you," Zoey said, scratching Harley's head as she eased him away from the table.

Everyone knew my dog wasn't allowed to have table scraps, but it didn't stop him from using all his cute begging techniques to get someone to give him a bite of their cheesecake. Not that they ever did. My favorite was when he combined a groan and a whimper, then acted as if he hadn't eaten in days, maybe even weeks.

"Now that we know Myles didn't disappear off his boat, it rules out the accidental death theory reported by the police," Vincent said

I leaned forward and snagged a napkin off the pile to

spread across my lap. "Zoey, while you were picking up tidbits about Myles, did anyone happen to mention how he died?" I didn't think anyone in law enforcement would release those details, but it never hurt to check.

"There was a lot of talk about that as well, but no one knows for sure," Zoey said, swirling her fork. "How about you? Did you notice anything interesting after you found him?"

I shuddered. "The body was partially buried, and I didn't stick around to examine what I could see." I wasn't about to let the images of Myles's corpse spoil enjoying some cheesecake and pushed them from my mind.

Delia took charge of serving. "Brinley, what would you like?" she asked after opening the box and exposing a large cheesecake; one side plain, the other covered with chocolate shavings.

"Chocolate, please," I said, holding out a plate.

Vincent didn't indulge in the more decadent desserts like the rest of us and was the only one who chose a slice of the plain.

Not long after we'd all settled back in our seats and were silently munching away, Myrna said, "That explains why Landon showed up at the crime scene."

No one had asked a question, so I wasn't sure what made her think of the sheriff. "For those of us who haven't lived here very long," I said. "Why is that relevant?"

"He and Myles were best buddies," Myrna said.

"Unlike Carson, there's a good possibility he won't be objective and search for the truth during the investigation," Vincent said, then stuffed another bite in his mouth.

"Should Landon even be allowed to work on the case if he was close to the victim? Wouldn't that be considered a conflict of interest?"

"It might be, but I doubt anyone will point it out to him," Delia said.

"Even if they did, he's not going to listen," Myrna said.

"Since we're on the subject of local law enforcement, I forgot to tell you that Carson called and asked me to come down to the station tomorrow," Delia said.

I narrowed my eyes at my aunt. She rarely forgot to tell me things unless it was on purpose. "Why does he need to speak with you? He already gave all of us his,"— I made imaginary quotes with my fingers—"don't-get-involved-with-my-case speech."

Delia's cheeks flushed. "It might be because I had lunch with Myles."

Another detail she'd failed to mention. After my aunt had divorced Uncle Craig, she'd relocated to Hawkins Harbor. I'd already moved away from home and lived in a larger city. Other than phone calls and text messages, I'd only seen her when she came to visit me.

I didn't pry into her personal life because I figured she'd let me know if she was dating anyone serious.

Hearing that she'd gone out with a recently murdered man was a little unsettling. I didn't want to discuss how upset I was that she hadn't shared the information with me in front of the others and planned to talk about it with her later.

"Landon's probably the one who told Carson to question you about your association with Myles," Myrna said, then scowled at my aunt.

"Why would he do that?" I asked.

"He's held a grudge ever since I refused to go out with him when I first moved here," Delia said.

"He can't honestly be angry enough to blame you for Myles's death, can he?" I asked. It was obvious that Delia and the others didn't think very highly of Landon. I wasn't willing to make any personal judgments about the man until after I'd met him. I was protective of my aunt, and the more I learned, the more difficult it became not to form negative opinions.

"You should've refused to go out with Myles as well,"

Myrna snapped. "I told you the man was a piccolo."

Before I could ask Myrna to explain why she thought Myles was a musical instrument, Delia sighed. "I believe the word you're looking for is gigolo, and he wasn't one of those either."

"You can't deny that the man had quite a reputation with the ladies." Vincent glanced in my direction and wiggled his brows. "If you know what I mean."

Grasping his meaning hadn't been hard, but I couldn't help wondering how Landon felt about his friend's reputation with the female populous. Law enforcement officials weren't exempt from committing crimes. Maybe the sheriff deserved a spot on the suspect list.

"I was well aware of his reputation," Delia huffed. "We weren't going out, and it wasn't a date."

"Then what do you call being seen having lunch with him in the deli a few doors down from his shop?" Myrna asked.

"Having lunch," Delia said. She glanced at all of our expectant faces. "Fine," she sighed. "It was right after you called to tell me you were visiting." Her gaze landed on me, along with a heart-warming smile. "I was out shopping and passed Myles's shop. I thought it might be nice to buy you a souvenir to take home with you. When I went inside, he was on the phone exchanging heated words with someone."

She held up a hand. "And before you ask, I couldn't hear what was said, and I don't know who he was talking to. I got the impression whatever they were discussing was something serious. When Myles turned on the charm and asked me if I'd join him for lunch, my curiosity got the better of me."

Delia might have been trying to fulfill an inquisitive need, but maybe the conversation had been more important than she'd realized. Perhaps it had something to do with Myles's death. Maybe the person he'd been speaking with had been the killer. "Did you learn anything about the call?" I asked.

"No, he refused to discuss it." Delia scowled. "He was more interested in discussing his divorce and how he was having a hard time dealing with being alone. After that, he spent most of the time talking about fishing and trying to get me to go see his boat."

"I'll bet while Myles was trying to get you to go to the marina, he forgot to mention he'd tried the same thing on some of the other older single women in town," Vincent said.

Delia tsked. "No, he didn't, but for clarification, Myles and I didn't get involved. I didn't see his boat. There was no kissing or anything else for that matter. Other than being a jerk, he certainly didn't do anything that would make me want to kill him."

I took a moment to process their conversation and the ramifications of my aunt now being a suspect in a murder investigation simply because she'd had lunch with the dead guy. "Carson didn't specifically tell you that you had to come alone, did he?" I asked.

Delia shook her head. "No."

"Good, then I'm going with you." Being protective of my aunt and showing support was only one of the reasons I wanted to go with her. Carson would most likely be tight-lipped if I asked him any questions about Myles's death, but maybe I'd be able to glean some information anyway.

I also wanted to meet Sheriff Lennox to determine if he'd added Delia to the suspect list out of spite or if he truly had a reason to believe she'd ended his friend's life. Even though I knew she was innocent, small-town gossip had a way of taking information and expanding it in the wrong direction. I didn't want anyone to assume she was guilty and decide to do something about it. The only way to do that was to find the culprit responsible for Myles's death.

"Am I right in assuming the HHSS is going off-line to

investigate Myles's murder?" I ran my gaze across each of their faces, noting the confirming grins. Trying to talk them out of it would be futile. Helping and keeping them from getting into trouble was my only option. Making sure my aunt didn't get blamed for something she didn't do was a strong motivator.

I finished the last bite of my cheesecake, then set my plate with my crumpled napkin on the coffee table. "If we're going to figure out who killed Myles, then I think it's important to figure out where he was killed."

"I agree," Vincent said.

"If he did supposedly start out on his boat, then somehow ended up in the water, how did his body find its way to the beach? And who buried him? There are plenty of places that don't get much traffic, so why that particular area? Was it something significant to the killer or a convenient place to hide him?"

I also wondered if whoever put Myles there wanted him to be found or to remain hidden. Had the storm ruined their plans?

"Those are good questions," Zoey said. "But how did they get Myles to the beach without being noticed?" After taking a swallow of water, she added, "Surely, the killer hadn't stuffed Myles in the trunk of their vehicle. Someone would've noticed them dragging a body from the parking lot to the area where you found him."

"Maybe they lured him to the beach, then clocked him over the head with a shovel," Myra said, bringing her fist down on the table for effect.

Harley lifted his head and groaned.

"Sorry, boy," Myrna said.

We already knew the killer had dug a hole for the body. I wasn't going to dispute that there'd been a shovel or something similar near the crime scene at some point. The hole hadn't seemed very deep, but I didn't think it was done by hand. The location wasn't that far from the water. Maybe some of the sand covering the corpse had been eroded by waves.

"They could've gotten Myles to that spot during that first storm. If I remember correctly, there'd been a lot of rain the same day Myles's disappearance had been reported." I stared at the wall, trying to recall all the details printed in the newspaper article. "I don't think the storm was as severe as the one we had last night."

"Since he was buried, we can rule out floating ashore with the tide," Vincent said.

"If they drove his body to the burial site, then how did his boat get out in the middle of nowhere?" Delia asked. "It would also be helpful to know if it was anchored or drifting when the authorities found it." The newspaper article had been vague about that detail.

"It's possible the killer moved the boat, which means they had to know which vessel belonged to Myles," I said.

"Does that mean the person we're looking for had been on Myles's boat?" Zoey asked.

"Either that or they're familiar with the marina," Vincent said.

"Without any real information, we could be speculating all night," I groaned. "It might be easier to figure out the how if we narrowed down who his enemies were."

Vincent choked on the bite he'd taken. "That's a long list," he rasped after smacking himself in the chest.

Zoey hopped up and walked over to the board in the corner. After selecting one of the colored markers, she wrote "Suspects" near the top, then asked, "Who do you think we should include?" She uncapped a black marker. "Do you think I should put Delia on the list?"

"No," we all said in unison.

Zoey lowered the hand holding the marker. "Geez, it's not like I wasn't going to draw a line through her name."

"I heard some of the women he dated had boyfriends," Myrna said. "One or two of them might have been married." A good deal of Myrna's information was derived from people, or rather her gossipy friends who lived in or near the Promenade.

Myles had disappeared from his boat shortly after I moved to town, so I never got a chance to meet the man. I wasn't going to be any help with developing a list. "Did you happen to get any of their names?" I asked.

"Not really, but I know someone who might be able to tell us who they are," Myrna said.

"Let me guess," I said. "We'll need to make a trip for pet supplies, won't we?" The last time we needed information, I'd learned that Leona, the owner of Pemshaw's Pet Boutique, was a good resource for information. The shop was pet friendly, which meant we could take Harley with us. If I purchased a few supplies, no one would have a reason for questioning our visit.

Myrna bobbed her head. "Yes, and while we're there, I need to pick up some pellets for Ziggy."

Myrna adored her pet and had happily treated me to pictures of the black-and-white guinea pig every week since I'd arrived.

"Did you want to come with us?" Delia asked Vincent.

He harrumphed. "You know I don't have any pets, nor do I have any interest in getting one. You girls go and tell me what you find out."

I knew Delia was teasing him because he'd recently told us about the fish he'd had as a child. He'd taken the creature's short life as a sign that he shouldn't invest in any future aquatic or furry pets.

"Zoey, how about you?" I asked. "Did you know Myles well?"

"No, he didn't hang out with my crowd, but I knew who he was because I'd seen him at some of the community center functions."

The retirement center sponsored a lot of events like game nights and dances that they opened to the public for a fee. Zoey was attractive. If Myles hadn't shown any interest, he must've preferred middle-aged women, which would help narrow down the suspects once we figured out who they were. The killer was most likely a man, but I wasn't going to dismiss the possibility of a scorned woman being responsible. Not until we'd gathered more details about his demise.

"I doubt Carson will be forthcoming with anything, but maybe we'll know more after we talk to Leona," Delia said.

"We can only hope," I said.

CHAPTER SEVEN

The novelty surrounding the nearby crime scene had diminished by the next day. It seemed that without a body, people lost interest. Personally, I was glad I could take Harley for a walk on the beach without worrying about stumbling over a corpse.

Business at the Bean had returned to normal. Other than an occasional tourist, who stopped to take pictures, the yellow strips of police tape seemed to have blended into the scenery.

I wasn't generally superstitious, but the first thing I did after arriving at the shop was check the aquarium for signs of new belly-up bobbers. I breathed a relieved sigh when I saw that all the fish were alive and swimming happily around their home.

Delia had called Carson to tell him she'd be by to see him midafternoon.

The town police station was a white, single-floor building with dark blue trim. The lot wasn't full, so we could park near the front door. Inside the reception area, a middle-aged woman sat at a desk behind a rectangular L-shaped counter. Her dark hair was pulled into a neat bun at her nape.

She was busily typing on a computer keyboard and stopped to glance in our direction. Her dark eyes sparkled with recognition, and she smiled. "Delia, how are you?"

"Fine," Delia said, placing a hand on my arm. "Gretchen, I'd like you to meet my niece, Brinley."

"Pleasure," Gretchen said. "Your aunt talks about you all the time."

I shot a side-long glance at Delia. "She does, huh?"

"Mostly to give us updates on your move," Gretchen said, her chair squeaking as she pushed to her feet. "I'm sure she's told you how happy she is to have you here."

"Yes, frequently," I said, which was the truth. Each complimentary sharing I'd received was accompanied by a hug, some even tighter than the daily ones I received from Myrna. I wasn't prone to crying, but having someone else tell me how much my move truly meant to my aunt had me blinking back the moisture building in my eyes.

"How's Archer enjoying his semi-retirement?" Gretchen asked. "I'll bet he's already headed off on one of his fishing trips, hasn't he?"

"Yes, he left a couple of days ago," I said. I still hadn't heard back from him and tried to keep the concern out of my voice.

"I understand there was quite a bit of excitement on the beach yesterday," Gretchen said. "I would've stopped by, but I had to work. And it was crazy here." She rolled her eyes. "I couldn't get any work done because the phones were ringing all morning, with everyone asking the same questions. Did I know someone found a body, and did I know who it was yet?" She paused to take in a breath. "Rumor has it you were the unlucky person who reported finding it."

"I'm afraid so," I said. Carson didn't seem like the type to toss out information. My money was on Douglas being the source of the so-called rumor.

"Not a good ending for Myles." Gretchen leaned forward and rested her elbows on the counter. "Between you and me." She glanced back and forth, apparently checking to ensure we were alone. "I'd heard he was into some shady stuff and figured it was only a matter of time before, you know…" She made a slicing motion across her throat.

"What kind of bad things?" I asked.

She straightened and shrugged. "Don't rightly know, but I heard it wasn't good."

I raised a brow at Delia, who gave me an understanding look. Just because Gretchen had heard the same tidbit of information we'd gotten from Zoey didn't mean it was accurate. It only meant the news had traveled throughout the community. The data wouldn't be substantial until we figured out precisely what the 'shady stuff' was. Hopefully, our upcoming visit with Leona would be more helpful.

Getting details from Carson would be close to impossible, but Gretchen didn't seem opposed to sharing. "I don't suppose anyone's confirmed the cause of death yet, have they?" I asked.

"Won't know until after the autopsy," Gretchen said.

Did that mean she'd be willing to share the information once she found out? I didn't want to jeopardize her job by questioning her where someone could walk in and hear her giving out vital information. Delia and Gretchen seemed to be good friends, so maybe getting my aunt's perspective on how to proceed would be a better way to go.

"Anyway, what can I help you with?" Gretchen asked.

"I have an appointment with Carson," Delia said.

Gretchen scrunched her nose. "Nothing serious I hope."

"No, I'm here for a chat." Delia made it sound like coming by the station was part of her regular routine. My aunt would know better than I did when not to divulge information that could find its way to members with gossip connections.

"Why don't you wait over there," Gretchen said, pointing at a wooden bench pressed against the wall near the entrance. "I'll let Carson know you're here."

We'd barely taken a seat on the hard wood when footsteps echoed from the adjoining hallway.

"Good afternoon." Carson saw me and added, "Ladies." Delia hadn't told him I would be coming along. He recovered his brief moment of surprise by forcing a smile. "I appreciate you coming in."

"Not a problem," Delia said.

I was still annoyed that my aunt had been summoned to the station and wasn't going to agree that I was okay with the inconvenience until I'd heard what Carson had to say.

"Please, follow me." He led us down a hallway and past an area with several desks. "We'll have more privacy in here." He motioned for us to enter a small room with a rectangular table in the center of the floor. It was definitely an interrogation room, adding to the unease I'd felt since we'd entered the building.

Delia and I settled into the two chairs sitting side by side on one side of the table. Carson closed the door and sat across from us.

"I assume you've already heard that the man you found was Myles Mumford," Carson said.

He couldn't have known about the chatter Zoey had overheard at the cheesecake shop. But he'd grown up in Hawkins Harbor, so he was aware that news would spread throughout the community, no matter how hard the police tried to keep it a secret.

"Yes," Delia said, shuddering. "Such a tragedy."

I gave her arm a comforting squeeze, then asked Carson, "Have you found out how he died or how he ended up on the beach yet?"

"I'm afraid I can't share any of those details with anyone during an investigation," he said. A flicker in his dark eyes was the only indication I got that he knew something.

"Since you both spend a lot of time at Archer's place,

obviously for different reasons, can you tell me if you noticed anything out of the ordinary during the past couple of weeks?" Carson asked.

"Sorry, no," Delia said.

Being new to the area and focused on getting settled and learning my job, I didn't have time to pay attention to outdoor activities. Unless I'd actually seen someone digging a hole on the beach, nothing had seemed unusual. "Is that how long you think he's been there?" The thought of Myles being buried that long without anyone noticing was more than a little unsettling.

Carson furrowed his brow and ignored my question, which by my interpretation, meant that's exactly what he believed. "You both have good instincts about people. Was there anyone hanging around the Bean or the beach that you didn't think belonged?"

I couldn't think of anyone that gave me a bad vibe, so I shook my head.

"I'm afraid not," Delia said.

"Okay then." Carson swept his hand along the side of his head. "Can you tell me about your relationship with Myles?"

"Contrary to what *the sheriff* believes, there was no relationship," Delia said, her voice calm and without emotion. "We had lunch in town one time. I never went with him to see his boat. There was no kissing, and we certainly didn't have sex." She paused for a few seconds, then added, "If that's what you were alluding to."

If Delia was trying to embarrass Carson, she was doing a good job. The man was squirming in his seat. I had to bite my lip and glance down at my lap to hide my amusement.

"No, I...those details weren't necessary." He cleared his throat. "How well did you know Myles?"

Delia leaned back in her seat and crossed her arms. "I thought we just established the fact that we barely knew each other. And I certainly didn't know him well enough to want to kill him."

I couldn't blame my aunt for being angry. The idea that anyone would think she was capable of murder irritated me as well.

"Carson's only doing his job," I said to Delia. He could have gone to my aunt's house or questioned her at the Bean. Instead, he'd invited her to the station, minimizing the scrutiny she'd receive from others and doing his best to protect her reputation. "He doesn't believe you're guilty of anything." I pinned him with a glare. "Do you?"

"Brinley's right," he said. "As far as I'm concerned, this is only a formality."

"All right," Delia said, dropping her hands to her lap. "What else do you need to know?"

"I think that's it," Carson said. "If you think of anything that might help, will you let me know?"

"Of course." Delia pushed out of her seat.

My aunt might be willing to share important information with Carson, but I didn't think it would be until after she and her friends had researched it first.

Once we exited the room, I glanced across the open area furnished with several desks and spotted Landon standing in an office doorway and scowling at us. After our so-called interrogation and the way he glared at my aunt, I was convinced that Myrna had been right, that questioning her hadn't been Carson's idea.

CHAPTER EIGHT

My trip with Delia to see Carson lasted about thirty minutes, leaving us enough time to pick up Myrna, then stop by my aunt's place to get Harley before walking to Pemshaw's Pet Boutique.

I couldn't stop thinking about the apparent grudge the sheriff still had over my aunt's rejection. Even if the circumstances were innocent and hadn't led anywhere, going out with one of his good friends wasn't helping the situation. I wondered if Landon would continue looking at Delia as a suspect or put aside his personal feelings and search for the real killer.

Even if he changed his focus, I didn't think it would matter to my aunt and our friends. They were all avid sleuthers and, when presented with a new mystery, whether real or imaginary, wouldn't stop until they'd solved it. I had to admit, I was too invested now to let it go either.

I pushed the glass door open and walked into the shop, hoping we'd get better information during our talk with Leona. She'd been helpful the last time my aunt and her friends decided to play detective.

One-half of the shop was designed to accommodate all

types of grooming needs, including baths, hair, and nail clipping for dogs and cats. The other half contained shelves stocked with a wide variety of pet care products. One entire wall was dedicated to fish and filled with rows of active aquariums, the dwellers both tropical and saltwater.

"Hey," Leona called out, giving a brief wave as she walked toward us with a boisterous bounce in her step. Her curvy figure filled out a uniform made up of black pants and a short-sleeved pink top that zipped along the front and had two large pockets below her waist. The blonde shade of her hair was created by a professional stylist and held away from her face with a pair of combs.

"Hey back," I said, returning her infectious smile with one of my own.

Harley did a little doggy dance and swished his tail, happy to see her. Especially after she grabbed a treat resembling a dog bone out of a container sitting near a check-out counter and held it out to him.

"Are you all right?" Leona asked as she ushered us to a nearby area with no customers. "I heard what happened." She tsked. "How horrible to take a walk on the beach and find...well."

I still shuddered every time images of Harley tugging on Myles's arm replayed in my mind.

"It's why we're here," Myrna said. "We need your help because it looks like Landon thinks Delia's involved." I'd heard the disgruntled comment before, but today, sarcasm laced her words. Not surprising since my aunt was one of her dearest friends.

"What's wrong with that man?" Leona snapped. "Anyone who's spent five minutes with you can't possibly believe you're capable of doing that to Myles."

"Jealousy makes people do things they wouldn't normally do," Myrna said.

I couldn't argue with her logic. That particular emotion had altered the course of my life. I'd gotten lucky and couldn't be happier about the change. Delia's circumstances were different and could go in a bad direction if the sheriff was convinced she killed Myles and was determined to prove it.

"What would he have to be jealous of?" Leona widened her eyes. "Oh, please tell me you weren't dating Myles too?" She'd made it sound like the man went out with a different woman every night.

"I went to lunch with him once, and *nothing* happened," Delia snarled.

My aunt was an intelligent woman and would never let herself be charmed into a bad situation. Every time she had to defend herself, her voice became more strained. I decided now might be a good time to change the subject and hopefully prevent Delia from having to do any more explaining. "Leona, do you happen to know if Myles was into anything shady?" I asked.

Maybe there was some truth to what Zoey had overheard at Tori's place because Leona didn't seem surprised by my question. Or maybe her interpretation of 'shady' had a different meaning than mine. "I guess it's possible, but I haven't heard anything significant." She tapped her chin. "You should talk to Ariel. She might know."

"Who's Ariel?" I asked since I'd never heard anyone mention the name before.

"Myles's wife," Delia said. "Their split up wasn't amicable."

"Things between them did get rather nasty." Leona slipped her hands into the pockets of her uniform top. "I also heard that Ariel accused him of cheating on her."

"Do you know the name of the so-called other woman?" I asked. Supposedly, wives generally knew when their husbands were being unfaithful. Unless Ariel was the type of person who made unfounded accusations, she was most likely right about Myles. It didn't matter how discreet people tried to be; there was always someone who noticed something.

"Not that I can recall," Leona said. "I guess it doesn't matter now that he's dead. Ariel won't have to worry about going through with the divorce."

"Wait," Delia said. "Are you saying they were still married?"

"Yes, as far as I know," Leona said. "Why? What did Myles tell you?"

"That their divorce had recently finalized," Delia said, her tone filled with rage. "If I'd known he wasn't telling the truth…" The rest of her comment never made it into the air. As angry as she looked, Myles was lucky he was dead; otherwise, I'm certain my aunt would've tracked him down and shared her thoughts on the matter.

It sounded like the man had a wandering problem long before he went out with Delia. Not to mention difficulty with telling the truth. I could only imagine how the conversation would've gone if she'd figured out he was lying during their lunch.

I agreed with Leona. It couldn't hurt for us to talk to Ariel. She'd be the one person in town who knew the most about him.

It also made her a suspect. Money and financial stability were always at the top of the list of motivating factors. How much would Ariel lose if the divorce had actually finalized? If things between the couple had turned nasty, it might have given her a reason to commit murder.

I didn't have an issue with going to her home, but there was a chance Carson would find out about the visit. Provided she didn't work in an office, it would be much easier and less conspicuous to question her if we showed up at her place of employment. "Do you know where Ariel works?"

"Oh, she doesn't have a job," Myrna said. "She and Myles owned a beautiful home in the Promenade. She was one of those pedestal wives."

Confused by her description, I glanced at my aunt,

hoping she'd provide a translation.

Delia blew out a breath. "I think you mean trophy wife, don't you?"

"What makes you say that?" Myrna snorted indignantly, then giggled. "I don't think Ariel won any awards for marrying Myles."

If Myles had been fabricating similar stories with other women in town, I was afraid the list of angry people would be endless. And questioning all of them wouldn't go unnoticed. Most of them would be upset, but I didn't think they'd all follow through with murdering him.

"Leona, do you know if there was anyone Myles was spending a noticeable amount of time with more recently?" I asked. "I mean before his reported accident."

"Not really," Leona said. "He wasn't a customer, so the few times I saw him were at a Promenade event."

"Excuse me," a familiar woman's voice came from behind me.

I turned to find Natalie Swafford, one of Leona's employees, inching toward us. She'd helped me a few times when I'd visited the boutique, but I didn't know her very well.

Natalie had been stocking shelves on the opposite side of the store when Delia, Myrna, and I arrived. She had an average build, and judging by the well-defined muscles that caused her uniform to fit snugly, I'd bet she had a membership at a local gym.

Her stealth was admirable. I hadn't noticed that she'd moved to the end of the aisle closest to where we were standing until she'd spoken. My suspicion that she had a habit of eavesdropping was confirmed by the way Leona scowled at her.

Natalie ignored her boss and continued, "I couldn't help overhear you ask about Myles."

Delia knew the townsfolk better than I did, so with a subtle lift of my chin, I motioned for her to handle the interruption.

"Is there something you wanted to tell us?" Delia asked.

"Well," Natalie said, drawing out the word as if she were about to reveal a high-security secret. "If you want to know what was going on in Myles's personal life, then maybe you should talk to Sherry."

"Sherry who?" Delia asked.

"Berkleman," Natalie said. "She's been spending a lot of time with Myles on his boat."

Was it possible this Sherry person was the woman Ariel thought was having an affair with her husband?

"And where did you hear that?" Myrna said. She tended to take all gossip she acquired as fact, so I was surprised to hear the skepticism in her tone.

Undaunted, Natalie lifted her chin. "I didn't hear it from anyone. I work part-time for my dad and saw her myself."

I hadn't visited the town's marina yet but knew that Dean Swafford's tackle shop was located nearby. As inquisitive as Natalie was, which was a nicer way of saying she was downright nosy, it was possible she saw everyone coming and going from the place.

It was too much to hope that Natalie wouldn't go around telling people that we were asking a bunch of questions about Myles. That kind of rumor, even if it was true, wouldn't take long to get back to Carson and the sheriff. Even so, I did my best to minimize the gossip. "Thank you for appeasing my curiosity," I said. "We've taken up enough of your time, and I don't want to keep you from your work."

"Yeah, sure." Natalie glanced at Leona, then picked up the box she'd left on the floor as if it weighed almost nothing and headed for another aisle.

Before we had a chance to continue our conversation, a woman possessing a haggard parent appearance approached Leona and asked, "I hate to interrupt, but can you help me find some food for my son's pet turtle?"

"Sure," Leona said, then turned to us. "I'll talk to you all later."

"Did either of you know about Sherry?" I asked once Leona and her customer were out of hearing distance.

Myrna shook her head.

"No, this is the first I've heard about it," Delia said.

"If they were seeing each other, they were doing a good job of hiding it." Myrna pushed on her glasses and wrinkled her nose. "Maybe she's the reason Ariel and Myles were getting a divorce."

"I was thinking the same thing," I said. If Natalie's information was correct, then it looked as if we'd need to talk to Sherry. I didn't think working out the details in the middle of the pet shop was a good idea. "We'll have to see what Vincent thinks." We'd planned to meet at his place later for dinner to share any information we'd gathered.

Harley spent most of his time during our conversation patiently sitting on the floor next to my feet. The dog was tenacious when he thought there'd be more treats coming. Now that Leona had gone, he was up, sniffing and pacing.

"I'll be right back. I'm going to grab some snacks for Harley," I said, then headed for the pet food aisle.

CHAPTER NINE

After leaving Delia and Myrna to chat about whatever plotting they would pull me into later, I made my way to the back of Leona's shop with Harley padding next to me, occasionally stopping to sniff the floor.

He wasn't a finicky eater, but he did have his favorites. I found the brand of treats he liked on an endcap near the pet food aisle. "Which do you prefer? Chicken or beef?" I held up a bag of each to show him, but when I looked at the spot on the floor where he'd been moments before, my dog was nowhere in sight.

His leash was looped around my wrist, the end closest to his collar stretched around the frame supporting the shelves. I'd been so preoccupied with reading product labels that I hadn't noticed he'd gone exploring. Luckily, he wouldn't get far unless he performed a magic trick and escaped from his collar.

I peeked around the corner and found him nosing through the contents of a hand-held shopping basket someone had left on the floor. He latched onto a bag of dog biscuits and pulled them out of the basket. Apparently, he didn't want to wait until we got home to have a snack, not when he could take someone else's.

"Harley, no." I used a commanding tone but kept the volume low so I didn't draw the attention of other customers. People were notorious for misinterpreting situations, and I didn't want anyone to assume I was mistreating my pet. Least of all, the basket's owner.

Most of the time, I didn't have any problem getting him to mind, but today he interpreted my grab for the bag as foreplay to a game and sidestepped out of my reach. "Drop it," I said, hoping that using a sterner voice would let him know I was serious. When that didn't work, I reeled in the leash so he couldn't get away.

Once I had the bag, I examined it for tears and was relieved that I didn't find any. I was about to admonish Harley with the threat of obedience school when I heard a familiar voice say, "That's the one."

Feeling like a thief who'd been caught in the act, I quickly practiced an explanation in my mind as I spun around and searched for the source of the person speaking.

I saw Ellie Poverly standing at the other end of the aisle. The elderly woman had a bob-style cut, the strands equally mixed with brown and silver. She had one hand on the bar of a shopping cart with a white plastic basket that had black paw prints randomly scattered along the outside surface. Clasped in her other hand was a leash for Bruno, her Chihuahua, who nervously made circles on the floor next to her.

My racing pulse slowed when I realized she wasn't talking to me but was giving instructions to the tall man pulling a bag of dog food off the top shelf. "There you go," he said and placed the bag in her cart.

He had sandy blond hair and blue eyes, and his cheeks formed dimples when he grinned. "Did you need anything else?"

"If you wouldn't mind, I could use a box of those doggy biscuits too." Ellie smiled and wiggled her finger as she pointed.

"Not at all." He turned and reached for the top shelf again. It was hard not to notice his muscular frame or how his jeans clung nicely to his backside. Guilt swept through me when I realized Ellie wasn't the only one staring at the handsome man with appreciation.

"Hi, Brinley," Ellie said. "Have you met Dr. Walsh yet?"

"No," I said, hoping the ogling I'd given him had gone unnoticed.

"You can call me Jackson," he said in a deep voice laced with an appeal that rivaled his good looks. He took a few steps forward and held out his hand. His skin was warm, his grip firm. As I shook his hand, I wondered how many other women in town wished they could catch a cold or flu bad enough to warrant a visit to the man's office.

I knew he couldn't read my mind, but the direction of my thoughts caused heat to rise on my cheeks anyway.

"You're Delia's niece, right?" he asked. "The one who took over managing for Archer?"

"Yes, but how did you know?" I asked. I definitely would've remembered if I'd seen him at the Bean or we'd met somewhere in town before.

"I'm your aunt's vet," he said.

Delia hadn't mentioned having any appointments for Luna lately. I was going to strangle her if she'd made a matchmaking visit to see him.

"Myrna told me when she brought Ziggy in for his checkup."

That was worse. Myrna had pictures of Delia and me on her phone and had probably shown them to him during her visit. I groaned and dropped my head, trying not to think about what else they'd discussed during their conversation.

The community's newest vet was also on the list of possibilities Delia and her matchmaking friends had mentioned during my vacation. According to Leona, pet sales had increased shortly after his arrival. After meeting him in person, I understood why. Not only did he score in the extremely gorgeous category, but he also had a genuine charm that was hard to resist.

Now that we'd been introduced, and with the high probability that Jackson and I would inevitably run into each other again, escaping gracefully would be impossible. Unless I wanted to give up shopping at the pet boutique, which I didn't, I'd have to suffer through more embarrassing moments.

Jackson must have sensed what I was thinking. "Don't worry," he said with a wink. "No dark secrets were divulged, and if they were, no one will ever hear them from me."

"You should make an appointment for Harley to see him," Ellie said. She glanced at my dog, whose gaze had shifted from the treats I clutched to my chest to her Chihuahua.

"Bruno just loves him," Ellie said, snatching the dog off the floor and snuggling him. "Don't you, boy?" The dog whimpered, but I couldn't tell if it was because he understood her and agreed or if he didn't like being squeezed.

"I can see why." The words slipped out before I could stop myself. I hated that my inside voice had a mind of its own and needed to be heard. At the rate my face was overheating, my skin would resemble a sunburn in no time. I contemplated if sticking my head in one of the fully functioning aquariums lining the wall would help or make things worse.

Jackson grinned, then picked up the basket sitting near my feet on the floor. His attempt to save me from further embarrassment didn't last long. I held out the bag of treats. "I believe these are yours." I glanced down at Harley, the culprit behind my predicament, who now presented an adorable picture of innocence. "I'm afraid my dog doesn't understand personal boundaries when it comes to treats."

Jackson tossed the bag in the basket, seemingly

unbothered by the theft. "That's okay. My dog doesn't either."

"Brinley, are you ready to go?" Delia said as she rounded the corner.

"Almost," I said.

My aunt's blue eyes sparkled when she noticed who I was chatting with. "Hey, Jackson. I take it you've met my niece."

"I have," Jackson said. "I'd love to stay and chat, but I need to get going." He gave me another one of his dimple-forming grins. "Brinley, it was a pleasure."

"For me as well," I said.

He took a step, then stopped. "I don't want you to think I'm trying to solicit your business or anything, but if you haven't decided on a vet yet, I'm pretty good with animals."

I giggled. "Actually, I scheduled an appointment at your clinic for later this week." I told myself the flutters in my stomach were caused by concern for my dog's welfare, not that I was looking forward to seeing Jackson again.

"That's great." Jackson's grin got even wider. "I look forward to seeing you, I mean both of you." He leaned over and scratched Harley's head on his way to the front of the shop.

"I think he likes Brinley," Ellie said once he'd disappeared from sight. "The man could have his choice of any woman in town, but that's the first time I've seen him show an interest in anyone."

I found her observation hard to believe. I thought about asking her how many women she'd seen him interacting with but didn't want to sound like I was scoffing at her.

"Was I imagining it, or did Jackson do that glance back thing when he walked away?" Myrna asked.

"What glance-back thing?" I asked. I hadn't wanted any of them to notice my interest and went out of my way not to stare at him when he left.

"You know, the thing guys do when they're interested in someone," Myrna said.

I found it hard to believe that my interest in Jackson was reciprocated.

"Where did you hear about that?" Delia asked.

"In one of those relationship magazines," Myrna said, her gaze switching from staring after Jackson to focusing on Delia's questioning look. "What? I read."

Before the conversation drifted in a direction where Ellie, Myrna, and Delia planned a future relationship for me, I changed the subject by asking, "Myrna, did you remember to get Ziggy's pellets?"

"Oh, no, I didn't," she gasped. "Thank you for reminding me." She turned and hurried away from us, calling, "I wouldn't have been able to face his cute little face if I got home without his food," over her shoulder as she disappeared down the next aisle.

"Don't let her fool you, Ellie." Delia laughed, motioning that it was time for us to go. "That guinea pig hasn't missed a meal his entire life."

CHAPTER TEN

Vincent dressing in a red Hawaiian shirt and khaki shorts was nothing new. Wearing a dark green apron with a dancing hamburger on the front and wielding a set of metal tongs over an outside grill presented a side to the grumpy old guy I'd never seen before.

As far as I knew, none of the properties in the retirement community had fenced-in yards, Vincent's place included. Since Harley usually did okay when left alone with Luna inside Delia's home for a couple of hours, I hadn't brought him along.

Zoey had a busy social life outside of work. Though she already had plans with a group of her friends and couldn't make it, she made me promise to catch her up on our progress in the morning.

Delia, Myrna, and I sat in the chairs around a table strategically placed in the shade provided by an awning that covered Vincent's backyard concrete patio. The awning extended far enough away from the house to provide protection from the weather for his grill.

The rest of his yard was covered in freshly mowed, lush green grass and a couple of small, randomly placed trees. The six-foot hedges running along both sides of his property created a natural fence and provided privacy from nosy neighbors.

After a busy day at work, followed by recon errands that included a lot of walking, it was nice to finally relax. My mind had other ideas. I couldn't stop thinking about all the tidbits I gathered about Myles. I struggled to piece them together and form a plausible reason why someone would want to murder him.

The smell of grilled chicken coated with a barbecue sauce Vincent had prepared himself wafted through the air and made my stomach rumble. "These are almost done," he said as he turned the meat for the final time.

"Great," Delia said, pushing back her chair. "I'll bring out the rest of the food."

"I'll grab the lemonade," Myrna said. "Unless someone wants tea." She gave each of us a glance.

"Fine with me," I said, getting up to follow them into the house and offer my assistance.

Four place settings with plates and silverware were already on the table, so all that was needed were the additional dishes we'd brought to accompany the meat. Delia had prepared a delicious-looking pasta salad. Myrna brought a vegetable platter. Because I didn't have time to cook and didn't want to arrive empty-handed, we'd stopped by Tori's place and grabbed another cheesecake. The non-plain half was topped with a strawberry drizzle.

Vincent was the first to break the silence after we'd filled our plates and settled into our seats to eat. "Did you find out anything interesting?" He didn't need to expound on his inquiry. We all knew he was asking about the information we'd gathered on Myles.

Myrna waved a carrot stick in the air. "Leona thinks we should talk to Ariel."

As far as I knew, I'd never met the woman. A lot of the people who came into the Bean were locals. I recognized them by face, but I didn't necessarily know their names unless they'd gone out of their way to introduce themselves.

"That makes sense," Vincent said. "Even though she's Myles's ex-wife, she'll still be a person of interest for the police."

"Only Ariel never quite made it to the ex-wife status," Delia said, her sarcastic tone relaying her continued annoyance with Myles's fabrication.

I wanted to tell her not to take it so personally. From what we'd heard so far, it sounded like he'd used his duplicitous skills on quite a few women.

"What?" Vincent asked.

"If the information Leona gave us was accurate, then it seems the divorce never happened," Myrna said.

My mouth watered as I sliced a sliver of meat off a chicken breast. It bothered me that Myles went out of his way to convince the ladies in town that he was now single. Other than the obvious, which equated to satisfying sexual needs, was there another more nefarious reason for the fabrication?

It would be difficult to figure out his motivation until I acquired more information. Instead, I focused on what we needed to do next. "Since Ariel doesn't work, does anyone have an idea on how we can run into her without making it look intentional?"

We'd done the same thing when we needed to talk to Ellie after she'd been robbed. Running into her had been easy since she took Bruno on a walk in the park every day.

"Sometimes she volunteers to help Avery with the events at the Promenade," Delia said. She got up and went inside, returning a few minutes later with a colorful flyer.

While she was gone, I took a couple bites of chicken. The sauce Vincent had made was a delectable combination of tangy and sweet.

"Let's see what they've got scheduled for the rest of the week," Delia said, pulling back one of the trifold edges.

As often as she attended the center's activities, I was surprised she didn't have their calendar memorized.

"Don't bother," Myrna said. "The boat race is tomorrow afternoon." She pressed her hands together and rubbed them enthusiastically.

My aunt tapped a spot on the flyer. "You're right."

"I'll bet anything Ariel will be there," Myrna said.

"Are you sure she won't be staying home to mourn?" I asked. Ariel and Myles might have been going through a divorce, but surely she must have cared about him a little.

"I doubt it. She never misses a race," Myrna said without hesitation. "Benjamin is competing, so I need to be there."

Benjamin was her nephew and had recently been promoted to manager of the Promenade. The thought of letting Myrna go by herself worried me. What if she switched modes from spectator to investigator? There was no telling what kind of trouble she might cause if she decided to interrogate Ariel in front of a crowd.

"Racing, huh," I said, smiling. It had been years since I'd been to a boat competition. Most likely because Delia and her ex-husband, Craig Danton, had been the ones who'd taken me. Unless an activity or event helped her social presence, my mother never showed any interest in attending. "Do you mind if I tag along?"

"I don't have any other plans and wouldn't mind going as well," Delia said. "Vincent, how about you?" She shot him an inquiring look laced with insistence.

"I suppose I can spare a few hours." Vincent might act like his time was precious and better spent doing something else, but I hadn't missed the hint of a smile. He wiggled his finger at Myrna. "No complaining or heckling the other racers if Benjamin doesn't win."

"What are you talking about? I would never..." Myrna's feigned innocence earned her identical scoffs from Delia and Vincent.

She leaned closer to me and muttered, "They're only giving me grief because I told them Ariel cheats."

I understood how emotional a competitive situation

could get, and since I'd never been to a race with the group, I chose to remain silent on the subject.

Myrna would rant if allowed, so Vincent dismissed her comment and asked, "What else did you find out during your clue-gathering expedition?"

"We chatted with Gretchen at the police station," Delia said. "She seems to think Myles was into something shady, but she had no idea what it was."

"Maybe there was some truth to what Zoey overheard at Tori's," Vincent said. "It wouldn't hurt to do some online checking and see if I can come up with anything."

"Great idea," I said. If the information existed, Vincent was the one person who'd be able to find it.

"Not bad for our first day of sleuthing," Myrna said, making a mock toast with her glass of lemonade before taking a swallow.

She was right. We'd done fairly well collecting puzzle pieces, but it annoyed me that we weren't any closer to finding out what happened to Myles and why.

With new plans in place, everyone went back to eating. I was about to take a bite of my salad, then remembered we hadn't discussed what we'd learned about Sherry. "How well do you guys know Natalie?" I asked, still not sure if she was a reliable source.

"Natalie who?" Vincent asked.

"Swafford," Delia said. "The young gal who works for Leona."

"Never met her," Vincent said.

Not knowing her was understandable. Vincent had no pets, so he wouldn't have a reason to visit the boutique unless one of his friends persuaded him to go with them.

"Not well, I'm afraid," Delia said. "I only talk to her when I stop by the pet shop."

"Same here," Myrna said.

"Why do you want to know?" Vincent asked.

I set down my fork and leaned back in my chair. "She went out of her way to tell us she saw Sherry Berkleman going out to Myles's boat with him."

"At the time, I thought she was being her nosy self, but now I wonder if she was telling the truth," Delia said.

"How about her father?" I asked. "Is he known to exaggerate information?" Even though Dean came into the Bean regularly, I couldn't recall ever seeing any of them socially interacting with each other. I was a decent judge of character, and based on my encounters with Dean, I didn't think he embellished information. Though some people possessed the skill of turning word manipulation into a natural talent.

"I don't know him either," Vincent said. "Archer's mentioned him a time or two whenever he discussed fishing. I believe Dean owns a bait and tackle shop near the marina."

"I've met him, and he seems like a nice enough guy, but you never can tell for sure," Myrna said, raising a brow. "But I know a way we can find out."

"And what would that be?" Delia asked.

"We stake out the marina." Myrna flashed us a mischievous grin.

"Or we could visit Dean's shop and chat with him," Delia said.

"Which might make him suspicious since none of us fish and have no reason to be hanging around the marina," I said.

"If we're back to using my suggestion, then I'd like to volunteer to pick out the snacks," Myrna said.

I'd developed quite a few diplomatic skills at my old job. To keep Myrna's feelings from being hurt, I said, "As much fun as your idea sounds, I'd rather not risk Carson catching us."

"We could talk to Sherry," Vincent said.

"Yeah, but what if Natalie was mistaken," I said, not wanting to inadvertently accuse a person I didn't know of something they hadn't done.

"Then talking to her would be embarrassing for all of

us," Delia said.

"So now what?" Myrna asked.

As I contemplated her question, I pushed the last remaining mouthful of pasta around on my plate. I couldn't shake the feeling that Myles's boat played an important role in the mystery behind his death.

When the police first thought Myles's death was an accident, would they have done a thorough search for clues? Was it possible they'd missed something?

Now that his body had been discovered on the beach, would local law enforcement consider taking another look at the vessel? Landon probably wouldn't, but Carson might, but there was no way he was going to tell us if he found anything.

When I looked up from frowning at my plate, Delia, Myrna, and Vincent were staring at me expectantly as if I had all the answers. Rather than let them down and tell them I didn't, I blurted out the first thing that popped into my mind. "We need to find out what happened on Myles's boat."

CHAPTER ELEVEN

When Delia, Myrna, Vincent, and I piled into my aunt's car, I'd expected the drive to end near a large body of water with a dock lined with boats. Not the pond adjacent to the park near the Promenade. "I thought we were going to see some racing," I said as I exited the vehicle.

"We are," Myrna said, slipping her arm through mine. "Come on." She led me from the parking lot toward a sidewalk running parallel to the pond.

More cars were pulling into the lot when we arrived. Other people, the majority of them retirees who most likely lived in or near the retirement community, were walking in the same direction Myrna was taking us.

"There's Benjamin," Myrna said, releasing my arm and taking off without waiting for the rest of us. She didn't exactly run but moved her arms and legs like a power walker. Myrna stood a few inches over five feet. Her nephew had to be a good foot taller, but it didn't stop her from throwing her arms around his neck for an affectionate hug.

He was standing next to a folding table with tool kits, a radio control, and a special mount containing a miniature racing boat. On our way to reach them, we walked past several other tables, and the owners I presumed would also be competing. Their boats had all been painted with an artistic flair, which seemed to be predominantly an animal theme. One was covered with the spots of a jaguar, another had a tiger's black and orange stripes, and the third resembled a zebra.

I glanced over my shoulder at Delia and Vincent, who kept pace behind me. "Why didn't you tell me the boats were motorized miniatures?"

"Myrna thought it would be a nice surprise, and we didn't want to ruin it for her," Delia said.

"This is great," I said. "And it looks like it will be much more fun than watching the full-size racers."

Benjamin was leaning over his boat, pointing something out to Myrna, and looked up from what he was doing and grinned. "Hey everyone, I'm glad you could make it." Short brown hair stuck out from beneath a cap like Myrna was wearing.

"You must be Brinley." He wiped his right palm on his thigh-length shorts, then offered his hand for me to shake. "I'm Benjamin, but you can call me Ben if you want."

Myrna swept her hand over the table. "And this is the boat we're cheering for." Benjamin's boat had a sleek design with a narrow front end to help it skim along the water. Instead of racing stripes, the dark green exterior was painted with alligator scales.

Myrna reached into a cardboard box under his table and pulled out three hats identical to the ones she and Ben were wearing. "Here," she said, handing one to Delia, Vincent, and me. "These will help with the sun, and everyone will know whose team you're rooting for."

Seeing how much supporting her nephew meant to Myrna, I couldn't tell her I wasn't normally a hat person. "Thanks," I said, slipping the cap on my head.

Even though Vincent rolled his eyes when Myrna wasn't looking, he plopped the hat on his head and gave the bill a tug, settling it on his forehead.

"Don't let her intimidate you." Ben frowned at his aunt. "You can root for whoever you like."

"Don't be silly," Delia said, slipping her sunglasses back on after adjusting her cap. "Of course, we're cheering for you."

I didn't know much about radio-controlled boats, but it looked like it required some skill. Maybe even a moderate learning curve, at least when it came to maintenance. "Do you do this often?" I asked.

"Not as often as I'd like because work keeps me pretty busy," Ben said. "I belong to a club that meets weekly, only at a different location. This is the first time the Promenade has sponsored an event. We're hoping to interest the hobbyist in the senior crowd. Maybe get some of them to become members."

What Ben and his fellow boating enthusiasts were doing was admirable. Sometimes people who'd spent their lives putting all their efforts into a job had difficulty getting used to retirement. Getting them involved with a competitive group was a great way to keep them socially active.

"Once the race is over, a few of us will stay around to answer questions," Ben said. "We also have some extra boats for those who want to dabble…if you're interested."

I could definitely see the appeal. My life was pretty busy at the moment, and I didn't need a new hobby. That didn't mean I wasn't willing to enjoy some play time and take a boat for a test drive. Not wanting to commit in case something came up and we couldn't stay, I said, "I might do that, thanks."

"Hey, Ben," Avery Noonan, the event coordinator, said as she hustled toward us. Her blonde hair was pulled back in a ponytail beneath a navy blue cap with the words "PROMENADE" embroidered in capitalized black letters across the front. The black and white striped referee apron and the thinly twined braid and whistle draped around her neck left no doubt that she was officiating the event.

Avery paused to inhale a breath. "I thought you should know the sailboats are almost done, and you and your group can get started." She pointed her clipboard towards a spot farther down near the water's edge where a group of people stood operating controls.

I'd been too busy admiring the colorful racing boats and chatting with Ben to notice that several small motorized sailboats were out on the water at the other end of the pond. Or that two round, white buoys had been placed in the water a distance apart and barely bobbed on the water's calm surface.

Avery turned to the rest of us and grinned. "Thanks for coming. We have extra chairs for spectators if you didn't bring any of your own. We also have a refreshment stand with beverages and snacks."

"I'll let everyone else know what to expect," Avery said to Ben, acknowledging he was her boss and she had every intention of doing a good job for him. To the rest of us, she said, "You all enjoy the race", then turned and scurried off toward another group of new arrivals.

I had a hard time leaving things unfinished and wouldn't be able to relax during the race until after I'd completed the reason I'd come here in the first place. I gave Delia a gentle nudge and asked, "Is Ariel here?"

"Over there." Delia glanced over her shoulder at a table that had recently joined the others. "Come on, I'll introduce you."

After wishing Ben good luck, we returned to the sidewalk with Vincent and Myrna tagging along, equally eager to assist with our newest search for clues.

Ariel appeared to be in her mid-fifties. She wasn't much taller than Myrna but judging by the tight fit of her hip pack, she had more layering around her middle.

She stopped rifling through her toolbox when she noticed our approach. "Myrna," Ariel rasped, then forced a smile at the rest of our group. Her dark eyes gleamed with the same kind of challenging glare rivals shared with each other before entering a competition.

"Ariel," Myrna replied with an equally sarcastic tone.

Apparently, the rivalry between Ariel and members of Benjamin's team, which had quickly increased by three, wasn't new.

I didn't think we'd get any information out of Ariel if she was locked in a glaring contest with Myrna. Fortunately, my aunt was thinking the same thing. She placed a hand on her friend's shoulder and said, "Why don't you and Vincent see if Benjamin needs any help. Or better yet." Delia unzipped her hip pouch and pulled out some cash. "Get us all something to drink and grab some chairs before they're all gone."

Myrna snatched the bills from her fingers but didn't look happy about being dismissed so Delia and I could question Ariel. Vincent, taking a conciliatory role, draped his arm over Myrna's shoulder and said, "You know, I think Zach would love to have one of these caps." He touched the bill of the one on his head.

Zach was Vincent's grandson and a whiz at solving online murder mysteries. He didn't live in town, so the few times we'd gotten stuck and needed his expertise, we'd done it via a conference call.

"Do you think so?" Myrna asked, all signs of irritation fading from her voice.

"Yep," Vincent said. "Do you suppose we could get one for him now so I don't forget later?"

Myrna could be unpredictable, so I waited for her and Vincent to reach Ben's table before turning to Ariel. "I like your racer." Her boat's design was similar to the others I'd seen. Only hers had a hot pink exterior covered with flamingo feathers. I didn't comment on the fact that she'd coordinated her clothing; a pale pink T-shirt and matching cap.

"Thanks," Ariel said. "And you are?"

"Oh, this is my niece, Brinley," Delia said.

"It's nice to meet you," Ariel said. She'd responded

pleasantly, leading me to believe there wasn't any competitive angst between her and Delia.

Remembering that Ariel had recently lost someone she cared about, even if I'd been informed it was in the past, prompted me to offer condolences. "I'm sorry about—"

Realization flickered in Ariel's dark eyes, and she interrupted me before I could finish. "Oh, my goodness, you're the one who found Myles's body, aren't you?" She didn't appear distraught in the least, only curious. Was Ariel's lack of caring because of the emotional strain caused by going through a divorce or because she had something to do with her husband's death?

"Yeah." It felt awkward not knowing what else to say, so I stood there and waited.

"I know everyone thinks I should be upset and stay at home mourning his loss," Ariel said. "I feel bad that he's dead, but the truth is, Myles and I grew apart years ago. Besides, I did my grieving the first time the police told me they thought he was dead."

"You mean when everyone assumed he'd gone overboard," I said.

"Exactly," Ariel said. "Nothing's changed other than finding out that his death wasn't an accident, and I now have a body to bury."

Those seemed like pretty significant changes to me, but everyone dealt with loss differently, so I wasn't about to disagree with her. "I take it Carson has been by to see you."

"He has, but he wouldn't tell me how Myles died, only that he'd been murdered," Ariel said.

If nothing else, the deputy was consistent in maintaining confidential information. "Yeah, us neither," I said, hoping the more I commiserated with her, the more she might be willing to share with us.

"If you must know, I kicked Myles out six months ago after I learned he'd been cheating on me." Ariel's expression transformed into a combination of hurt and anger.

I pressed my lips together, trying to pretend that I hadn't already heard the same bit of gossip.

"No," Delia gasped. She was way better at pretending to be ignorant than I was.

"As far as I know, he's been living on his boat ever since," Ariel said.

From what I'd learned about the man, I didn't think it was his first indiscretion. As much as I wanted to know for sure, I didn't want to insult or cause Ariel any additional humiliation by saying something.

"Do you know who he was seeing?" Delia asked.

"No," Ariel snarled. "Carson asked the same question, but I don't know how it's relevant." She paused. "Unless you think the woman, whoever she is, had something to do with Myles's death."

The last thing we needed was for Ariel to start a gossip campaign that led to making accusations about any of the local female populous who'd been seen in his company. My aunt included.

"I think Landon has it in his head that I was dating Myles," Delia said.

I hadn't planned on mentioning that detail and was glad my aunt had been willing to share.

"That's ridiculous," Ariel said, then burst into laughter.

"I thought so." Delia chuckled and pressed her hand to her chest.

I glanced at the other racers and noticed Avery stopping to chat with each of them. It wouldn't be long before she headed in our direction, and I still had a few unanswered questions I wanted to ask. "Did you know rumors were going around about Myles being involved in some unsavory activities?" I wanted her to think I was on her side and tried to sound sympathetic rather than judgmental.

"Really?" Ariel asked, her body tensing.

"You don't think his business was in trouble, do you?

And that's why…" I purposely left the sentence unfinished, hoping Ariel would be forthcoming if she knew something.

"I don't know," she said. "Myles never discussed the shop finances, even when we were still together." Ariel tucked a loose curl behind her ear. "I wouldn't be surprised if a jilted husband or boyfriend started the rumor to get back at him for messing with their wives or girlfriends."

Having been married to Myles, Ariel would know better than anyone what he was capable of. If I couldn't find anything to substantiate the shady business rumor, I'd have to dispense with my theory about him being killed in a deal gone wrong.

I was also beginning to believe Ariel might be innocent of murdering her husband, but if she stood to lose things during the divorce, it would still give her a motive. We might not get another chance to find out the truth. Rather than use a subtle approach, I blurted out what I wanted to know. "You know there are some people who think *you* offed your husband."

"Well, they'd be wrong," Ariel huffed. "I will admit there were times over the years when I wanted to strangle him, but I'd never hurt him. Working on the terms of our divorce might have been unpleasant, but a few weeks ago he agreed to let me keep the house."

I assumed Myles's death also left her with his business and other assets. "What about the boat?" I asked. I still wondered if the vessel held a clue to what happened to her husband. "Have you taken it out since, you know…"

Ariel pointed at the pond. "I'm afraid that's as close as I like to get to the water. I have trouble with motion sickness, so I've never been interested in spending time on the ocean. Once things settle down, I'll probably sell the boat."

By 'settle down', I assumed she meant when the police found out who'd killed her husband.

Ariel shifted her gaze between Delia and me. "Do either of you know anyone that might be interested in buying it?"

I remembered the board Archer had mounted near the shop's front door for people to list miscellaneous sales and apartment rentals. "Not at the moment, but you're welcome to post a flyer at the Bean," I said. "If you don't mind, we'd love to check out the boat." I glanced at my aunt, hoping she'd play along.

"Absolutely," Delia said.

"We could even take pictures for you while we're there. If anyone asks, we can give them our honest opinion and hopefully push along a sale."

Word of mouth was a powerful thing. It was also a plus when you lived in a town that attracted tourists and where boating and fishing were popular.

"Wonderful," Ariel said. "I don't have a key to the boat with me, but Dean over at Swafford's Bait and Tackle always kept an extra key for Myles. Tell him you have my permission to go onboard. He can call me if he has any questions."

CHAPTER TWELVE

Having Myrna and Vincent accompany Delia and me to the marina had sounded like a great idea until the topic of the previous day's race came up.

"No way should Benjamin have taken third place," Myrna said. Delia had offered to drive, and Myrna was sitting in the passenger seat behind her. "Ariel cheated. I know she did."

Ariel's flamingo had kept pace with Ben's gator most of the race. The only reason she'd pulled ahead during the last lap and taken second place was that Ben's boat experienced a mechanical problem or an operator distraction issue. I'd noticed Ben glancing in Avery's direction a few times and wondered if he had any interest other than being her boss.

"Does that mean the guy operating the zebra racer cheated too because I remember him beating both of them?" Vincent said.

The harrumph and glare he earned from Myrna made me glad I was sitting in the front with a view of the seat they shared in the back.

I returned to staring out the window and mentally reviewed what I wanted to accomplish. First up was confirming the reliability of Natalie's news about Sherry. After learning from Ariel that Myles lived on his boat, coupled with Natalie's nosiness skills, there was a good chance what she'd told us was accurate. With any luck, her father paid attention to the activities in the marina, and hopefully, a conversation with him would gain us the additional information we needed.

Since Natalie worked at the bait and tackle shop part-time, it would be awkward if we ran into her again. Especially, if she caught us asking more questions about Myles.

I was afraid if Zoey or I called and Dean answered the phone, he might recognize our voices from all the times he visited the Bean. Delia was more than happy to contact the store and pretend to be one of Natalie's friends to get confirmation that she wasn't working before we made our trip.

After passing a sign pointing to the Hawkins Harbor marina, Delia pulled off the main road and turned onto a side street leading into a parking lot.

Off to the left was a network of wooden-planked docks extending out over the water where numerous boats of various styles and sizes were moored. Beyond that was the ocean, where I spotted several more boats on the horizon.

Up ahead and positioned near the water's edge was a sizeable slate-gray building with a slanted roof. Extending from the corner of the building to a post near the walkway was a sign in dark blue letters that read "Swafford's Bait and Tackle." Below that hung another sign that said, "Marina Office."

If Dean's business shared a building operated by the marina, did that mean he owned both? If he did, he'd have access to the whole place. It was hard to know if obtaining the data would be relevant in helping us find the person responsible for Myles's death. Time spent playing an online mystery game taught me that even the subtlest details could provide a much-needed clue and should never be dismissed.

While I pondered the new development, Delia parked in a far corner away from other vehicles, where we had a relatively unobstructed view of the boats and Dean's shop. I undid my seat belt, shifting so I could face everyone. "Are we clear on the plan?"

"Yes," Myrna said, bending forward to pick up the bag of snacks sitting by her feet, then setting it on the seat between Vincent and her. Even though we'd explained the plan to her several times, she was convinced our outing would turn into a stakeout. "I still don't see why we can't all go with you. I make one heck of a good wingman."

"She's going to ask questions and get the key to Myles's boat," Vincent grumbled. "Not look for cute guys to pick up."

"There's no reason she can't do both." Myrna pulled a bag of red licorice from the sack and waved it in front of Vincent's face.

The odds of me finding an eligible bachelor, provided I was actually looking for one, hanging out in a bait shop couldn't possibly be in my favor. Rather than attempt to discourage her matchmaking, which would likely backfire on me, I hid my amusement and said, "I appreciate the offer, but like we discussed before, Dean might be less likely to chat if we all showed up in his shop together."

It was too bad Archer hadn't returned from his boating trip. He and Dean were friends and had fishing in common. We could've sent him in to do the information recon that we needed.

"Fine," Myrna said, tearing open the bag of licorice. After Vincent pulled out a piece, she made the same offer to Delia, then settled back in her seat. With everyone happily munching on candy, I got out of the car and readjusted the pack on my hip before heading for Dean's place. I was a person who used a purse before I moved in with my aunt. It didn't take me long to see the benefit of traveling without a strap slung over my shoulder. A strap that tended to slip down my arm during many of my daily activities, like taking Harley for a walk in the park.

Pressed up against the front of the building was a rectangular bench and a little further down was an ice machine. I noticed a set of gas pumps mounted on a concrete base near a black and yellow guard rail that ran along the edge of the dock where motorized boats could obtain gas. Since Dean's shop was the only one I'd seen in the area, I wondered if supplying fuel was also part of his business.

I pushed open the metal-framed glass door and stepped inside. The interior was noticeably cooler than the humidity I'd left outside. I glanced around, searching for Dean, taking a moment to peruse the store.

The majority of the poles had to be for deep-sea fishing. A portion of one wall was covered with long pegs used to hang a selection of T-shirts in varying colors. Some were stamped with the marina's logo, and others had cute fishing artwork and slogans. The shelves in the glass display case beneath the cash register were lined with all kinds of bait and lures.

Judging by the assortment of goods and the store's layout, I'd say Dean ran a decent business. Besides taking care of everyone's fishing needs, he had an aisle filled with snacks. He even had a cooling unit sitting in the corner filled with a wide selection of bottled waters, energy drinks, and sodas.

I saw another sign for the marina office. It was smaller than the one outside and posted above a doorway in the middle of the wall to the left.

A young guy, maybe in his early twenties, was helping a customer. He turned and glanced in my direction with a welcoming smile. "I'll be right with you," he said, then pulled a small bag from a peg attached to a display and showed the older man next to him the contents.

"Brinley." I heard my name and glanced behind me to find Dean entering the room through the doorway linking the office with his shop. He didn't bother to hide his surprise. I was one of the last people he'd ever expect to see in his store. "How are you?"

"Fine, thanks," I said. "And you?" I was anxious to ask my questions and get Ariel's key but knew I'd have to utilize pleasantries to extract any information.

"Keeping busy." He nervously pulled the dark green cap sporting a fishing logo off his head, then swept his hand over the dark strands before replacing it. "I didn't know you had an interest in fishing."

"Actually, I don't," I said. "I ran into Ariel at the Promenade yesterday."

"The boat races, right?" he asked.

"Yeah." I nodded. "Did you go?" I'd been reasonably thorough in checking out the attendees in case anyone I'd learned was associated with Myles had made an appearance. I hadn't seen Dean, but that didn't mean he hadn't been there.

"I'm afraid my daughter Natalie couldn't make it in, so I ended up covering her shift," he said.

I didn't know the dynamics of their relationship, but I recognized disappointment when I saw it. I'd seen the expression on my mother's face repeatedly over the years.

"That's too bad," I said. "It was the first time I've ever been, and I had a lot of fun." It was the truth, so it made discussing the topic easy. I preferred not to be dishonest if I could help it, but under the circumstances would resort to fabricating details if necessary. Sharing my enthusiasm was also a good way to get people to open up, which I desperately needed Dean to continue doing.

Tossing in a compliment or two never hurt either. "You have a pretty good location here. I'll bet you get quite a bit of traffic from tourists and the people renting slips for their boats."

"I do pretty well," Dean said, grinning. "You mentioned something about running into Ariel. Was that what prompted your visit?"

"Oh, yes." I nodded. "She said you kept a key for Myles's boat."

"I do, or rather the marina requires a key for all renters in case of emergency." His grin faded, replaced by a suspicious tone. "Why?"

"She's thinking about selling the boat, and I was hoping to take a look." Unless he asked, I was happy to let Dean assume I was interested in purchasing the vessel.

"No offense, but I can't give out keys without permission." Dean pulled his cell phone out of his pocket.

"Not a problem," I said, then patiently waited for him to make the call, hoping he wouldn't have trouble reaching Ariel. Since I hadn't wanted her to know the real reason behind inspecting Myles's boat, I didn't call to give her a heads up before we started our trip.

From what I could hear of Dean's side of the conversation, it sounded like Ariel had given her approval. "Thanks, and take care," Dean said. As soon as he ended the call and tucked his phone back into his pocket, he retrieved a set of keys from a drawer underneath the cash register.

I followed him to the doorway of the marina office and watched him open a cabinet mounted on the wall behind a reception-type counter. Inside the unit were numerous rows of pegs, many supporting small silver rings with keys and colorful tags containing names and numbers.

Keeping the key for the cabinet in a drawer where anyone could access it didn't seem very secure to me. It made sense if Dean couldn't be here all the time. No one could predict when a problem would occur and require the use of a backup key.

"Do you have to handle a lot of emergencies?" I asked, remembering what he'd said about the renters' keys. I took a few steps back so Dean could reenter the shop.

"Not very often, but it can get a little crazy once in a while."

"I take it being able to operate a boat is mandatory if

you want to work here," I said.

"It's not a requirement if they only want to work in the shop," Dean said. "But it is if they want to work for Hugh."

"Are you talking about Hugh Cooper?" I asked, unable to grasp a connection between the two men I couldn't recall ever seeing together in the Bean.

"Yes, he owns the marina," Dean said. "He requires all his employees to go through the boating safety program to get an education certificate. Natalie and I have been around boats most of our lives, and we've also gone through the program. Jeff here has a certificate as well." He hitched a thumb at the young man ringing up the order for the customer he'd been helping when I arrived.

Jeff concentrated on handing back change, but his grin told me he'd overheard the compliment. He looked too young and innocent to cause someone's death. With his sun-induced tan and extra highlights in his light brown hair, I'd bet anything that he spent most of his free time hanging out on the beach and trying to impress the girls.

With all the traveling Hugh did, it was a shock to hear he actually owned one of the town's prominent businesses. A business with connections to Myles's death.

Thinking about the beach reminded me of our group's discussion about the possible ways Myles ended up buried in the sand and his boat drifting a long way from the marina. I still wasn't willing to dismiss the vessel as an important clue. It meant the killer could be someone who knew how to handle boats and most likely possessed one of the certificates Dean had mentioned.

"Ariel mentioned that Myles was living on his boat," I said. "Do you know if he got many visitors before his...demise?" Since I didn't know for sure that Myles had cheated on his wife or that he'd been involved with someone before his death, I didn't want to publicly accuse him.

Dean snorted. "Is that your polite way of asking

whether or not he entertained a lot?"

"Maybe." I couldn't tell him I was searching for more names to add to the super sleuther's suspect list. "I'd recently heard that Sherry Berkleman had been out to see him a few times." I didn't mention Natalie specifically in case Dean had an overprotective fatherly nature.

"She wasn't the only one," Jeff said. "I saw Claire Tillerson spending some time with him as well." After Jeff's customer left, he'd leaned against the display unit with his elbows propped on the counter.

Dean had his back turned and hadn't noticed that his employee had listened intently to our conversation until he'd spoken. His reaction to hearing Claire's name was unexpected. His entire body tensed, and he fisted the key to Ariel's boat tightly in his hand.

It was obvious that he knew the woman, but how? And why did her many visits to see Myles bother him? With Dean's increased irritation, I was a little wary about asking him outright. Jeff might be forthcoming with the information, but I didn't want to get him into more trouble with his boss.

"Don't you have something you should be doing?" Dean asked Jeff.

"Uh, yep. A new shipment of bait arrived yesterday." Jeff pointed at one of the aisles. "I think I'll go get it and restock the shelf."

"Good idea." Dean waited until Jeff disappeared through the doorway leading to the back of the building, then turned his scowl on me. "Why all the questions about Myles?"

I had a feeling if Dean didn't like my answer, he'd personally hold the store's front door open while he asked me to leave. I took a few seconds to gather my thoughts, then said. "Partly because I'm the one who found him." Forcing a shudder hadn't been necessary. It was my body's natural reaction every time I conjured an image of Myles in my mind.

"And partly because his death wasn't an accident, and it bothers me that he was dumped near the Bean." I might only be the shop's manager, but I took pride in my job and had grown protective of the place. I also wasn't thrilled that Landon treated Delia as if she would suddenly become a serial killer.

Dean was a good customer, and I liked him. The last thing I wanted to do was upset him, but I'd watched plenty of crime shows to know that with enough circumstantial evidence, people could be convicted. I wasn't about to let that happen to my aunt.

He seemed to be giving what I'd said some additional thought. I couldn't tell if he was imagining what it would be like to come to work and find a body or if I'd missed a vital clue and was conversing with a murderer.

"I guess that's understandable," Dean said, holding out a key chain containing two keys. "If you're unfamiliar with boats, this one's for the ignition." He tapped one of the keys. "Which you don't have permission to use. The other one is for the cabin door."

Did he think I was going to steal the boat? "Okay," I said, tamping down the urge to roll my eyes.

Satisfied that he'd made his point, he relinquished the keys to my care. "The name of the boat is *Catcher's Delight*, and it's anchored on dock "E", slip fifteen. The information's also on the tag."

I confirmed what he said with a glance at the piece of paper slipped underneath the clear plastic in the center of the green tag.

"Take a left once you get outside. The numbers are all posted."

"I will, and thanks again for your help," I said as I pocketed the keys and headed for the door.

"Oh," Dean said before I could leave. "You'll need to bring the keys back when you're done."

After agreeing with a nod, I stepped outside, excited to share what I'd learned with the group. Other than the keys to the boat, I hadn't expected to gain much from my visit with Dean. Not only did I confirm the information Natalie had given me about Sherry, but I'd also learned about Claire.

Deep in thought and staring at the ground as I headed toward the parking lot, I hadn't been paying attention to what was in front of me when I rounded the corner of the building. Running into a wall of firm muscle made me falter. If Carson hadn't steadied me with his strong hands, I would've ended up on my backside.

"Brinley, are you okay?" He may have sounded concerned, but his frown said he wasn't happy to see me in a place I didn't usually hang out. A location associated with the case he was investigating.

"Fine," I said, taking a step backward when he released me.

"Are you here by yourself?" While he turned his intense dark gaze on the area behind me, which happened to be the front of the store, I gave the parking lot a nonchalant glance and saw Delia, Myrna, and Vincent quickly ducking down in their seats.

If I told him they were waiting for me in the car, he'd know we were here snooping for clues. I wasn't in the mood for one of his lectures, but lying would eventually come back to bite me in the bodily area he'd spared from greeting the concrete, so I glanced around and uttered, "Um."

"I didn't know you were into fishing," he said.

"I'm not. Ariel asked me to take a look at her boat."

He narrowed his eyes and crossed his arms. "Don't you mean Myles's boat?"

"Technically, it belongs to Ariel now."

I was sure the noise he made, a cross between a growl and a snort, was in lieu of admitting that I had a point.

"And why would she ask *you* to inspect her boat?" he asked.

I was happy to give him the same excuse I'd given

Ariel. "I ran into her at the Promenade yesterday, and during our conversation, the topic of the boat came up. She wants to post sales flyers in the Bean. Since she has trouble with motion sickness, I volunteered to take some pictures for her and answer questions about the boat's condition if any of my customers asked."

Carson might be on duty, but I didn't think personal business was a topic he couldn't discuss. "What about you?" I asked. I didn't dare ask him directly if he'd been following me, but I wanted to know if the inquiries I'd been making about Myles had somehow gotten on his radar. "Why are you here?"

"I'm following up on a reported theft," he said.

After recently being involved in uncovering a string of house break-ins, it was hard not to be concerned. "Should I be worried?"

"Not unless you own an outboard," he said.

"Seriously, someone stole a boat from the marina?" I didn't keep up on the statistics, but it seemed like a bold thing to do. "Does that happen often?"

He rubbed his nape. "More than you'd think."

My priority was supposed to be checking out Myles's boat. Once I realized my curiosity for details was getting the better of me, I stopped asking questions to get away from Carson before I gave away what I was up to. "I better let you get going then."

"You have a nice day, and try to stay out of trouble."

"Will do," I said, relaxing when his steps took him toward dock "A", and nowhere near where I was going.

CHAPTER THIRTEEN

It would've been nice to have Delia, Myrna, and Vincent helping me search the boat, but with Carson hovering in the vicinity, it was too risky. I knew they'd seen him and hoped they remained out of sight until he left the marina or I returned to the car.

Once I'd found dock "B", it didn't take long to locate slip fifteen. Based on the information I'd gathered from the people I'd talked to so far, the exterior image I'd conjured of the *Catcher's Delight* was pretty close. The boat wasn't rigged for fishing, but it was a little bigger than I'd imagined, though not quite as large and fancy as some of the other vessels I'd observed.

After checking out the upper portion of the boat, I unlocked the door and descended the few steps leading into the cabin area, which to me, ranked in the comfortably leisure category.

The sunlight filtering through the doorway behind me wasn't enough to provide decent visibility, so I felt around until I found a switch that activated overhead lighting.

It appeared as if the basic amenities were covered. The cushions lining the benches on either side of a table that had been laminated to resemble dark wood were a light beige. I wasn't going to take the time to check but assumed, with some rearranging, that the area could be transformed into a bed. There was a small kitchen with a sink, a miniature refrigerator, and upper and lower cabinets.

I was anxious to open drawers and check every inch of the place but figured I'd better take the pictures I promised Ariel first. I pulled out my cell phone, selected the photo app, and started snapping. I would send what I thought was the best to her later.

I even took a few shots of the bathroom and included the inside of the shower stall. Tanks were a great place to hide things if you thought like a criminal. I was glad the toilet's plumbing system wasn't the same as a house, making one less place I'd have to check.

I'd barely tucked my phone away and opened my first drawer when I heard a loud thud and what sounded like footsteps overhead. My pulsed raced, and I froze.

Why would someone else be walking around on the deck? Was it the person responsible for Myles's death? Was I right about the boat containing incriminating evidence, and the killer had returned to retrieve it?

What happened if they found out I was on board and decided that letting me live was too risky? Delia, Myrna, and Vincent were hiding in the car, too far away to know I might be in trouble.

I usually handled tough situations without panicking, but with all the data I'd been collecting lately and knowing that the killer could be someone I knew, my mind began filling with all kinds of scenarios. Scenarios that didn't end well for me.

The sealed rectangular windows were too narrow for me to squeeze through. The only other way off the boat was via the closed cabin door, and I'd be seen if I tried to sneak out that way. I was about to hide in the shower stall when I heard my aunt calling my name.

"Down here," I said, relieved that I wouldn't be facing

off with a killer. "How did you find me?" I hadn't given them the slip number for the boat, so I was glad to see them yet concerned at the same time.

Vincent patted his pack. "I used my binoculars to see which way you went."

"What about Carson?" I asked. "Did he already leave?" I dreaded what might happen if he caught them in the marina. If he wanted to be lenient, we'd all get another warning. If he didn't, then he'd drag us down to the station and subject us to an interrogation or decide we'd earned something worse. It was the latter that worried me, and I hoped they'd gone unnoticed.

"Uh, we don't know for sure," Myrna said.

"Why not?" I asked. They had a perfect view of the marina from where my aunt had parked.

"We were hiding," Delia said. "And when you didn't come back right away, we decided to come after you."

"We used stealth moves to get here, so I don't think he saw us," Myrna said.

I wasn't reassured. Myrna didn't possess any ninja skills. Even if she did, her bright yellow sneakers wouldn't have gone unnoticed.

"So," Myrna said, rubbing her hands together. "Did you find anything before we got here? Like the murder weapon or a bloody shovel?"

Though drowning or dying from a smack on the head were my two top choices, it was difficult to search for whatever caused Myles's death when none of us had any idea how he'd died.

"I don't think the murderer would've left his or her weapon laying around for the police to find. Not if they wanted everyone to think Myles's death was an accident," Vincent said, sneering.

"Hey, even killers get sloppy and make mistakes," Myrna said. "That's how they usually get caught."

"Vincent's right," Delia said. "What we need is a clue, something that got overlooked."

I wasn't a private investigator or driven by the belief that my searching skills were stellar, but I was happy they'd shown up to help. "I was just getting started. Feel free to take a look around," I said. "Just make sure to put everything back the way you found it."

While Myrna and Vincent lifted cushions to check the storage compartments built into the benches, Delia and I opened drawers and inspected cabinets in the kitchen area.

I was disappointed that none of us had found anything, but our trip to the marina hadn't been a total waste of time. "Do you guys know Hugh Cooper?" I asked. I still hadn't confirmed whether or not he was a resident. His visits to the Bean weren't frequent, but that didn't mean they hadn't crossed paths at some point in the past.

"Sure," Delia said. "He occasionally attends the Promenade events."

"I've talked to his mother a few times," Myrna said, scowling. "That woman has to be the most unpleasant person I've ever met."

"Why do you want to know?" Vincent asked, settling the last of the cushions back into place.

"Dean told me Hugh owns the marina," I said. "I guess he manages the place for him."

"That is interesting news," Delia said. "I thought he owned a business up north and only came here to visit his mother."

I went on to tell them what I'd learned about Sherry and Claire. "Hearing Claire's name seemed to upset Dean. Does anyone know why?"

"I'll have to confirm it with my sources, but I think the two of them were an item once," Myrna said.

I didn't completely trust the information she gathered from her so-called gossip connection, but to date, they'd been fairly accurate.

"We should have a chat with Sherry and Claire to see how close they were to Myles," I said. "That's assuming you know both women and how we can run into them without being obvious."

"We know them," Delia said. "And we can definitely plan an accidental meeting."

My aunt's devious nature had me grinning.

"We should also find out if there was any brewing animosity between them and Myles," Vincent said. "It also wouldn't hurt to find out if they have alibis."

"Good point," Delia said. "The killer could easily have been a woman."

I had to agree since digging a hole wasn't that difficult. Given enough time, even I could manage one large enough to hide a full-grown person.

It was figuring out how the body had been moved that currently troubled me. Maybe it hadn't been an issue for the killer if they knew how to operate boats and used a small one to access the beach via the water.

"I don't think there's anything here," Myrna said as she crawled backward from underneath the table. I had no idea what she thought would be hiding down there, but she earned points for being thorough. "A little help here," she said after making two attempts to pull herself up and failing.

It was time to go, and once Delia and Vincent got Myrna to her feet, I said, "Let me check outside to make sure Carson's not hanging around first."

After a quick peek, we made it back to the main dock. "Why don't you all head back to the car," I said. "I need to return the keys."

Other than a gruff thank you, Dean didn't have much to say, not that I thought he would after all the prying I'd done. I noticed Jeff hanging out near the gas pumps when I left the shop. The boat he'd recently fueled, rumbled, then pulled away from the dock.

Jeff seemed like someone who didn't miss much and might be willing to share a few more juicy tidbits with me. After glancing through the shop's glass door to make sure Dean wasn't watching, I strolled in his direction.

"Hi, Jeff," I said. "I'm Brinley. We spoke earlier."

"Yeah, I remember," he said, smiling. "Are you related to Delia Danton?"

"Yeah, she's my aunt."

"You kind of look alike."

It wasn't the first time I'd heard the comment, though I was curious to know how he'd made the connection since I couldn't remember ever seeing him before today, not even in the Bean. "How do you know Delia?"

"I help out at the Promenade sometimes," he said. "You get to know the regulars by name after a while." He shoved his hands in his pockets. "I know she and her friends are into a popular online mystery game and sometimes do their sleuthing off-line, if you know what I mean."

"I do," I said, wondering how Myrna, Vincent, and Delia would take hearing they'd developed a reputation. I wouldn't be happy if it was me, but they'd no doubt be thrilled.

"Am I right in thinking that you guys are trying to solve Myles's murder?" Jeff asked.

Before I could come up with something to dissuade him, he held up his hand. "It's okay. I won't tell anyone. I think I might have something that will help, but first, let me ask you how cool it would be to make the front page in the newspaper." Jeff made air quotes with his fingers. "Local business manager finds a body, then solves the murder."

I didn't think it would be cool at all, nor did I want the notoriety. "Awesome," I said sarcastically. "Now tell me what you know." I glanced toward the door of Dean's shop, raising my brow to let him know it wouldn't look good if his boss caught us chatting.

"Right," Jeff said, taking the hint. "It might not be anything, but a couple of days before Myles disappeared, he got into a huge fight with Hugh."

"Do you know what it was about?"

Jeff shook his head. "I was too far away to hear what they were saying."

"That's okay." I wanted to squeeze in a couple more questions before Dean came looking for Jeff, so I led with the most obvious. "Did you know Myles well?"

Jeff shrugged. "He was an okay guy. A lot nicer than some of the other renters."

"Besides Hugh, can you think of anyone else who might have had a problem with him?" I asked.

"Nothing out of the ordinary, and nothing so bad someone would want to kill him for it."

If he knew about Myles's overzealous dating tactics that resulted in disgruntled boyfriends and possibly husbands—a fact I had yet to confirm—he wasn't saying anything. "Thanks, Jeff. I appreciate the help."

"Hey," he called after I'd taken a few steps toward the parking lot. "If you guys solve the crime, promise you won't forget to mention my name for the newspaper article."

"I won't forget," I said and continued walking. I didn't have the heart to tell him there wouldn't be an interview.

I'd just settled into the passenger seat and closed the door when I received another jolt to my nervous system. Carson must have approached the car in stealth mode. I didn't see him until he rapped his knuckles on the glass and motioned for me to lower the window.

"Hey, Carson," I said. "Are you all finished with your theft problem?"

"Yes." He bent down so everyone else in the car would get a good look at his furrowed brows. "I thought you said you were here alone."

"Technically, I didn't say anything." Pointing out that he'd assumed I was alone would only irritate him more. "And you didn't ask me if I had anyone waiting for me in the car." Okay, so maybe I wasn't above antagonizing him a little.

"What were you *really* doing on Myles's boat?" he

asked.

Before Myrna got the chance to make a flippant remark about Landon and our attempt to remove Delia from his suspect list, I said, "Like I told you, taking pictures for Ariel."

Carson hadn't witnessed us rifling through the boat's interior, so he couldn't prove we'd ignored his earlier warning. I unzipped my pack and pulled out my phone. "I thought they turned out pretty good. Would you like to see them?"

Carson stayed silent for the longest time as if waiting for someone besides me to crack under his scrutiny. When no one did, he finally said, "No, but if I find out you were doing anything that involves my murder investigation, I won't hesitate to haul you all down to the station." He gave the hood a couple smacks, then strolled off in the direction of his vehicle.

Once my window was closed, simultaneous sighs echoed through the interior.

"That was close," Delia said, placing a hand over her heart, which was no doubt racing as fast as mine.

I fastened my seat belt. "We should go before he changes his mind."

Myrna giggled. "Best stakeout ever. And look, there's still some licorice left." She held out the bag. "Does anybody want some?"

CHAPTER FOURTEEN

The early morning crowd had come and gone. Things had slowed down inside the Bean enough for me to spend a few minutes out on the deck with Delia, Myrna, Vincent, and Harley. The handful of customers remaining were sitting at tables inside and wouldn't be able to hear our conversation.

"We already know that Myles and Ariel weren't originally from town," Vincent said, his gaze focused on the computer's screen. He rarely brought his laptop to breakfast unless he had something he considered critical to share. "I couldn't find anything online or via my sources that suggested he'd been involved in anything questionable or illegal."

After a busy day at work and our trip to the marina the day before, I'd been exhausted by the time my aunt and I returned to her place. Instead of having a group meeting to review the information we'd gathered, I'd opted for a quiet night at home to spend quality time with Delia and Harley.

"Well, that's not what I expected," I groaned and leaned back against the railing. Finding something scandalous to tie to the shady business rumor Zoey had provided would've been helpful and led to a motive for

Myles's death. "Maybe Ariel was right about a jilted husband or boyfriend being behind the rumor."

Delia snapped her fingers. "We should ask Zoey if she can remember what she overheard and from whom."

As if on cue, Zoey stepped outside with refills for everyone. "Whom what?" she asked as she replaced the empty cups on the table with new ones.

"Remember the night you stopped by Tori's place to get the cheesecake?" I asked.

Zoey nodded. "Uh-huh."

"You told us someone was talking about Myles's being into something shady."

"Yeah," Zoey said. "Why?"

"Can you remember specifically who started the conversation?" I asked.

"Not directly. A few people voiced their opinions on the subject, so I don't know where the rumor originated."

"That's too bad."

"It doesn't mean I can't find out who started it." Zoey gave everyone in the group a wicked smile, then went back inside.

"Oh, before I forget," Myrna said. "You'll be happy to know I heard back from some of my friends in the retirement community network." She smiled smugly. "I was right. Claire and Dean were indeed a thing for almost a year."

"Did anyone know why their relationship ended?" I asked. "Or if Myles had anything to do with it?" Would the loss of someone Dean cared about be enough motivation for him to commit murder?

"No, but everyone I talked to said the breakup was amicable and that they'd remained friendly afterward," Myrna said.

"So, where does that leave us?" Delia asked.

"I'm not sure," I said. "I'd thought about adding Dean to the suspect list the instant I'd learned he had access to the keys for Myles's boat, but now I'm not so sure."

Harley had been napping under the table until he noticed Douglas tromping across the beach to the place where he'd found Myles's body. He whined, jumped up, tail wagging, and pressed his nose through a gap between the wooden spindles along the railing. Barking wasn't his thing unless he considered someone a threat or he caught a glimpse of a stray cat, which generally turned out to be Quincy.

Delia shifted sideways in her seat to see what had caught everyone's attention. "It looks like the police are done with the crime scene."

"Do you think they found the killer?" Myrna asked, her voice laced with disappointment.

"I don't think so," Vincent said. "I'm sure we would've heard about it already if they had."

Carson might not be willing to share information with civilians, but I had a feeling Douglas might not be as tight-lipped as his boss. "I'll be right back," I said, hurrying inside. Zoey had the memory of a computer when it came to the favored drinks of the locals who regularly visited our shop.

I slipped behind the counter to where she was preparing an order and, in a low voice, asked, "What does Douglas Dankworth like to drink?"

When I reached the beach, Styrofoam cup in hand, I found Douglas removing the tape he'd strung the day Harley found Myles. "Morning, officer," I said as I padded across the sand.

He looked up and smiled. "Oh, you can call me Douglas."

"You guys work hard." I held out the cup. "I thought you could use a break." When he hesitated to take it, I added, "I promise not to tell Carson."

"Thanks," he said, confirming my assumption that he wanted to stay on the deputy's good side.

I waited for him to take a sip. "I hope I got it right. Zoey said you liked Mocha Frappucinos."

"She remembered what I like to drink?" He glanced fondly in the direction of the Bean as if Zoey would materialize any second.

"She sure did." I pointed at the tape no longer attached to the stake and dragging on the ground. "Are you opening up this part of the beach again?"

"Yeah."

"Does that mean you're done investigating Myles's death?" I asked. "Did you find the killer?"

"No way. Deaths like this take a lot of work and fact-checking." He glanced at the ground, then mumbled. "Or so I'm told."

"Do you at least know how he died?" I expected to get the same comment about not being able to discuss an ongoing case and was shocked when Douglas said, "Blunt force trauma."

When he realized he'd let a critical bit of information slip, he added, "And that's all I'm going to say."

"Blunt what?" I asked, slipping my hands in my apron pockets and pretending I had no idea what he meant.

My act must've been believable because he huffed, "Okay, fine. Myles was hit alongside the head with something heavy."

"Like a shovel?" I asked.

"That's one possibility." He shrugged. "We don't know for sure...yet." He took another swallow, closing his eyes as if savoring the taste.

When he opened his eyes and noticed me watching, his cheeks flushed a bright red. "Thanks again for the drink, but I should..." He wiggled his finger at the tape.

"Oh, no problem," I said. "I need to get back to work myself." I spun around and headed for the Bean, eager to tell everyone that we now knew what caused Myles's death.

Only my plans were delayed. When I got back to the shop, I noticed Hugh sitting at the counter by himself. After my talk with Jeff, I had some unanswered questions about Hugh and decided I might not get another opportunity to ask them.

"Where's your mother today? Is she all right?" Not out of politeness, but to confirm that she wasn't in the bathroom. The woman was my least likable customer, and I didn't want a repeat of the serial killer conversation we'd had the last time she'd stopped for coffee.

Hugh smiled. "She's fine. I was headed out of town again and wanted a coffee for the road."

He already had a cup and a plate with a partially eaten scone sitting in front of him, so I didn't offer to get his order. "I didn't know you owned the marina," I blurted out the item holding the top spot on my list. I could've worked in a few more social pleasantries before appeasing my curiosity, but I was afraid more customers would arrive and require my assistance.

If the topic seemed strange to Hugh, his expression didn't show it. "Mostly in name only," he said. "Dean Swafford takes care of the daily things for me, so I don't have to worry when I travel."

"So you don't own a boat?" I asked.

"Actually, I do. I have a rather nice sailboat, but it's docked in a marina near my home up north." He smiled. "Someday, if and when I decide to relocate here permanently, I'll use it to take a trip along the coast."

Moving onto the next item, I said, "I'm guessing you knew Myles Mumford then."

"Not well."

"I heard you got into a heated argument with him right before he disappeared."

Hugh tensed and straightened his shoulders, a crease forming above his brows. "Where did you hear that?"

"It's a small town. You can't go anywhere without someone passing along a juicy tidbit." Not that I believed every nugget of news I heard. I would've dismissed it if the information hadn't been connected with a man's death.

Being the owner of the place where Myles kept his boat, the same vessel associated with his disappearance, was too much of a coincidence to ignore. I needed to find out if Hugh had a motive to get rid of Myles or if he had a decent alibi.

"Yes, we had an argument, but I didn't kill him if that's what you're thinking. He was late with his slip rental for the second month in a row. "

"If Dean's managing things for you, why didn't he talk to him?"

"He did the first time, but the two of them have some history, and things between them got uncomfortable." He held up a hand. "And before you ask, Dean didn't share the particulars with me, and I didn't press him for them." He eyed me over the rim of his cup while he took a sip. "It's no secret that your aunt and her friends are mystery buffs and like to do some amateur sleuthing." He set his cup on the counter and smiled. "I assume you're asking me all these questions because they've roped you into joining them."

I released a nervous giggle, glad that his irritation at my nosiness seemed to have passed. "More like helping out to make sure they don't get into any trouble."

"If you're trying to get my alibi without asking directly, let me help you," Hugh said. "I left town right after my conversation with Myles and was gone for almost a week. I can show you travel receipts if you need them."

"Totally not necessary," I said, grinning. "I appreciate your candor and thanks for being such a good sport."

CHAPTER FIFTEEN

As I walked along the sidewalk leading to the main shopping area in town, I thought about the talk I'd had with Douglas earlier in the day. If Myles had died from a smack to the head like he'd said, then his killer could be a man or a woman. It wouldn't take much to swing a weighty object if you caught someone off guard.

Getting a heavy body to the beach might be more difficult for a woman than a man, but I didn't think it would be impossible. It was the reason I wasn't ready to rule out Myles's past girlfriends, or at least the two I'd heard about; Sherry Berkleman and Claire Tillerson.

It seemed odd that Ariel didn't know about them. Or maybe she did and hadn't wanted to share the information. But why would it matter now that her husband was dead? Unless denying their existence helped maintain her dignity and prevented additional gossip. In that case, I couldn't say I blamed her.

I'd already discussed stopping by the Shoreside Salon where Sherry worked after closing the Bean. Delia and Myrna volunteered to take Harley for a walk and meet me there. Social mingling or questioning when the gang was in sleuthing mode made Vincent uncomfortable, so he asked to be excluded from our outing.

He preferred going to a barber to have his hair done and had no use for a frilly feminine place. His words, not mine.

I stepped inside the reception area and was bombarded by the familiar smell of hair products and the sound of human chatter and hand-held hair dryers. The interior was done in shades of mauve and lavender. The individual stations and chairs were a dark gray.

"Good afternoon," the woman sitting behind the curved check-in counter said. Beauticians loved to show off their work on their clients and themselves. Her long black hair was cut in an angled bob and sported thin streaks of bright turquoise that matched the colors in the print of her dress. Though her mascara seemed excessive, the rest of her makeup looked professional and enhanced high cheekbones. "Can I help you?"

"Yes," I said, walking up to the counter. "I was hoping to see Sherry Berkleman."

"Do you have an appointment?" she asked, glancing at the computer screen.

Stylists who had a decent clientele could rarely fit someone in without them having to wait first. Based on Delia's and Myrna's complementary recommendations of Sherry's hair care skills, my plan was to meet the woman and, under the guise of scheduling a future session, ask her a few questions about her association with Myles.

"No, I recently moved to town and needed to find a new stylist." Once again, I was glad I could rely on the truth to further my conversation and said, "My aunt told me I should give Sherry a try, but I'd like to meet her first if that's all right."

"Of course, it is," a woman said as she approached me, her heels clicking on the smooth, gray-marbled floor tiles. Short blonde hair with soft curls caressed her shoulders, the strands along her forehead forming airy wisps above her eyebrows. "Who is your aunt?"

"Delia Danton," I said.

"I've done Delia's hair many times," Sherry said. "She is such a lovely person and couldn't be happier about you moving here."

"So I've been told." By pretty much everyone I'd met who knows my aunt. Hearing it again only reaffirmed that I'd made the right decision.

Sherry leaned over the counter to see the receptionist's computer screen. "It looks like I have some time available right now. I'd love to chat with you, but on one condition."

I didn't like how she eyed my hair as if it was a lump of clay that she wanted to mold into a masterpiece. "Which is?" I asked, certain I already knew the answer.

"You let me do something with this." Sherry reached out and touched a few of my strands.

The last time I'd been in a salon was before my vacation to see my aunt. I didn't think the condition was so bad that it warranted the scrunched-up face she was making.

"All right, but I need to let my aunt know first," I said, then pulled out my phone and sent a text to Delia that said, "Running behind, strong-armed into a haircut."

Receiving three emojis with smiling faces wasn't the response I'd expected.

"What name would you like me to use?" The receptionist held her hands poised over the keyboard, then glanced at her screen.

"Brinley," I said.

"Last name?" she asked.

"Brubaker."

She skimmed her fingertips across the keys and, after a few seconds, smiled. "Great, you're all set."

"My chair's over here," Sherry said, taking the lead. Once she had a cape secured around my neck, we were off to the shampoo bowl.

Other customers were getting their hair washed in the

sinks next to us. With the water running, I'd have to speak louder than I wanted, so I decided to wait until we returned to Sherry's station to ask about her connection to Myles. While she rambled about trivial topics, I relaxed and enjoyed having my scalp massaged and hair cleaned.

I'd barely settled into the chair's cushioned seat before Sherry said, "I heard about your discovery on the beach." She faced me toward her mirror, then toweled the excess moisture from my hair. "I knew Myles, and I can't imagine how awful it must have been to find his body like that."

It appeared that obtaining the information I wanted was going to be easier than I thought. "It was definitely an experience I wouldn't wish on anyone else," I said.

I watched in the mirror as she combed my hair, her focus on studying the strands and the outcome she wished to attain.

"If it's all right with you, I'd like to trim about a half-inch off the ends." Sherry gripped the hair on each side of my head near my cheeks and pulled it forward. "As well as a little feathering to enhance your facial features."

I appreciated that she was the kind of stylist that didn't take liberties without asking first. Her suggestions didn't sound too drastic, so I said, "Okay."

Sherry used the comb to section off my hair. After applying clips, she began cutting.

"I was at the marina the other day taking pictures of Myles's boat for Ariel," I said, then paused. I needed to be careful how I worded my questions. It was never a good idea to provoke someone wielding a pair of scissors. I didn't want to annoy Sherry and end up with a shorter haircut than we'd discussed.

"I know it's none of my business, but someone said they thought you and he were, you know…" I let the rest of the sentence hang in the air, giving her the opportunity to fill in any missing information. It was a slight fabrication, but I didn't think Sherry needed to know it was Natalie who'd offered her name during my visit to the pet boutique.

"This town has way too many nosy people," Sherry grumbled, then stopped cutting and made eye contact with me via the mirror. "Myles and I never...nothing ever happened between us. Ariel is a regular customer and a good friend. The only reason I agreed to meet with Myles was to see if I could find out the name of the mysterious girlfriend. I told him I wanted to learn how to fish, so he'd invite me to his boat."

"Did Ariel know?" I asked.

"Of course, she did," Sherry said.

It seemed Ariel was more devious than I thought. "Did you ever find out the person's name?"

"No," Sherry said. "Which is too bad because it would've helped with the divorce." She tapped the back of the chair by my shoulder. "Not that it will make much of a difference. I suppose Ariel will get everything now."

"You're probably right," I said.

With all my questions about Sherry's relationship with Myles answered, I spent the rest of my time in her chair chatting about the best places to eat and shop.

"All done," Sherry said as she removed the cape.

I twisted my head from side to side, taking a moment to admire her work. She'd done a fantastic job. "It looks great. Can I get a business card?"

"Absolutely," she said, then led me back to the reception area. "It was great to meet you." She handed me a card from one of the holders sitting in a line on the end of the counter. "I hope to see you again soon."

***

Delia, Myrna, and Harley were window shopping at the store next door to the salon when I stepped outside. "Hey, guys," I said, fluffing the ends of my hair.

"Very nice," Delia said.

"Told you Sherry was good," Myrna said, smirking.

Harley whined, so I knelt down in front of him. "I didn't forget you." I scratched his head and giggled when he got up on his hind legs and licked my face.

I pushed to my feet and asked. "Are you guys ready to head over to Claire's shop?" She was the only other person we knew of with a connection to Myles that we hadn't questioned. Even if we weren't searching for clues, after hearing that Claire owned Dreamy Delectables, I was looking forward to checking out the candy shop.

"Yes," Delia said, handing me Harley's leash. "Her place is a few blocks farther up and on the left."

"Did you learn anything interesting from Sherry?" Myrna asked after we started walking.

Harley paced happily next to me, stopping every so often to sniff whatever he found interesting on the sidewalk. "Believe it or not, Sherry wasn't dating Myles," I said. "She was conspiring with Ariel to find out if there was a mystery woman in his life."

Myrna snorted. "That sounds like Ariel, all right."

Delia rolled her eyes at Myrna, then asked, "Did she learn anything?"

"No," I said.

"Do we think it's possible that Myles wasn't the cheating husband Ariel made him out to be?" Delia asked.

A reputation for charming the ladies was hard to dismiss when my aunt was one of the women he'd tried to lure to his boat. "I don't know." Any further consideration would have to wait because we'd reached our destination.

The building housing Dreamy Delectables was hard to miss. The storefront was painted a shade of pink that reminded me of bubblegum-flavored chewing gum. The wood door and frame surrounding the glass panels were a darker pink bordering a shade of deep purple. A slanted white awning stretched along the front of the building and provided shade for the benches sitting on either side of the entrance.

Harley rarely gave me any trouble when we went for

walks, and I'd almost forgotten he was with us. The pet boutique was the only place I'd visited that allowed animals in the store. "Slight problem," I said, glancing down at him, trying to figure out a way to question Claire without taking him inside.

"You two go," Myrna said, motioning me to hand over the leash. "I'll stay out here with Harley."

"Are you sure?" I asked. Harley was low maintenance, but I didn't want to impose.

"Yep. Oh, and here." She slipped her hand into her pocket, pulled out some cash, and then handed it to me.

"What's this for?" I unfolded the crumpled five-dollar bill.

"You can't go inside and ask questions without buying something. You'll look too conspicuous. If you wouldn't mind, I'd like a package of red licorice whips or ropes, if they have them. If not, get me something sweet. No chocolate because it will melt before I get home." Myrna placed a hand on my arm when I turned. "Oh, and nothing sour. My tongue will be puckering for hours." She formed an "O" with her mouth, the wrinkles around her lips deepening.

Now there was an image I could've done without.

"Good grief, Myrna," Delia huffed. "Do you want to go yourself?"

"Nope." Myrna plopped down on the bench and pulled Harley onto her lap. "I'm good."

"This place is unbelievable," I said once Delia and I were inside. I inhaled deeply, enjoying the combined aromas of all the delicious goodies. The entire back wall was lined with shelves stocked with all kinds of packaged sweets. Thick pink and white stripes, starting at the ceiling and ending at the hardwood floor, served as a colorful backdrop.

Several round white display tables were positioned in the center of the room. Each one contained a circular unit comprised of numerous bins filled with different kinds of candy and a metal scoop. A couple other customers were milling about, oohing and awing like small children as they perused some of the shelves.

"It is, isn't it," Delia said. She'd been here before, yet her gaze sparkled with awe.

Now that I knew where the place was located, and after seeing all the wonderful things available, I planned to visit more frequently. That was unless we somehow managed to upset Claire to the point where coming into the shop made us both uncomfortable.

Since Myrna was nice enough to babysit Harley, I didn't want to disappoint her by getting distracted while talking to Claire and forgetting her licorice. I quickly found the display she'd mentioned and selected two long, red ropes.

There were only two people dressed in brightly colored uniforms, and neither of the women looked old enough to be the shop's owner. "Do you think Claire's here?" I asked Delia.

"Let's find out." She strolled toward the clerk working near the cash register. "Is Claire around?"

"She's in the back," the clerk said. She must have recognized my aunt from previous visits because she didn't ask any more questions. "I'll go get her for you." She walked around the counter and disappeared through a door marked with a sign that said, "Employees Only."

I didn't want anyone to overhear our upcoming conversation with Claire. "Let's move over here." I slipped my arm through Delia's, leading her to the shop's far end and away from other customers.

An older woman wearing a similar uniform followed the clerk into the room. She saw my aunt and smiled. "Hello, Delia." She watched her employee return to work, then asked, "How are you?"

"Great, thanks," Delia said.

I didn't think Claire would've answered truthfully if my aunt had asked her the same question. Either she had bad allergies, or she'd been crying. I was going with the latter since her makeup appeared fresh but didn't completely conceal the shadows beneath her dark eyes.

"I wanted you to meet my niece, Brinley," Delia said. "She's now a resident and staying with me for a while."

"That's great." Claire sounded sincere, but I detected a hint of sadness. It was as if she wished she could be somewhere else, possibly a place where she could mourn without anyone knowing.

I wasn't sure why the thought had popped into my head or why I suddenly had a strong feeling that I'd found the woman Myles was secretly dating and couldn't resist saying, "I'm sorry about Myles."

Claire's eyes snapped into focus, and she stammered, "What?"

"You were seeing Myles, weren't you?" I asked, trying to be sympathetic and persuasive, without sounding judgmental. "It won't go any further than us, I promise."

Claire blinked away the moisture building in her eyes and sniffed. "I guess there's no point in hiding it now that he's gone." If she knew I was the one who'd found him, she kept it to herself. "I want you to know that we didn't get together until after he and Ariel separated."

"So, why the secrecy?" I asked.

"Because of Dean and Natalie Swafford. I wanted to spare their feelings."

"I'm not sure I understand why you wouldn't want them to know," I said, pretending I wasn't aware of her relationship with Dean. I flashed Delia a look, urging her not to say anything either. We only had basic details, most of them hearsay, and I wanted accurate facts from the one person who could provide them.

"Dean and I dated for a while," Claire said. "We both realized around the same time that it wasn't going to work. Our breakup was mutual, but we were able to remain friends."

"How did Natalie handle it?" I asked.

"She and I were close, so naturally she was devastated. I think part of it was because she'd lost her mother at a young age and had a hard time coping with it. Dean mentioned that she'd had to see a therapist for a couple of years afterward."

Claire shook her head. "Natalie was determined to get us back together. She'd even resorted to asking me for lunch and inviting her father without letting either of us know the other was going to be there. I finally had to tell her it wasn't going to happen; otherwise, she never would've relented."

"How did she react when you told her?" Delia asked.

"She wasn't happy about it." Claire glanced at the floor, possibly recalling a troubling memory. When she raised her head again, she said, "At the time, I remembered thinking that she hadn't heard me, that nothing I said would get through to her."

"Did you ever tell Natalie about Myles?" I asked.

"No, but somehow she found out and confronted me about it, so I had to tell her the truth."

"And how did that go?" I asked.

"Surprisingly well," Claire said, though she didn't sound totally convinced.

I'd bet anything that if Claire took the time to analyze the conversation she'd had with Natalie she'd discover it hadn't gone as well as she'd thought.

CHAPTER SIXTEEN

I'd never been to a vet's office before, but the way my pulse raced, I'd have thought I was the patient, not Harley. Though I was pretty sure it might have had something to do with seeing Jackson again. Not that I would allow myself to consider the possibility. I was a realist, and a handsome guy like him, who had the majority of women in town vying for his attention, probably already had a gorgeous girlfriend.

When Myrna and Delia offered to tag along, I knew it wasn't based on generosity. I sensed a conspiratorial matchmaking adventure in the works and had refused them both.

Zoey was quite capable of handling things by herself after the morning rush, but with Archer still gone—a concern I'd shared with my aunt and been told not to worry—I hadn't wanted to leave her alone by taking off early. Most businesses were open until five, so any personal things I needed to take care of could be scheduled for later in the afternoon.

Harley and I arrived for his appointment fifteen minutes early and parked next to one of the two other cars in the lot. It looked like Archer wasn't the only one who'd renovated a family dwelling and turned it into a business. The building's exterior was a pale yellow, the two front windows trimmed with white and adorned with medium blue shutters. Mounted on the wall next to the main door was a sign painted in black letters that read "Hawkins Harbor Animal Clinic."

I clipped the leash to Harley's collar, then helped him out of my car. He danced around my feet, tail wagging. "I'll be honest with you, boy," I said, leading Harley to an area designated as an outdoor doggy facility. "This isn't going to be pleasant, but you've already met the vet, so it shouldn't be too bad. Jackson seemed like a nice guy to you, didn't he?" I hadn't expected an answer. I'd voiced the question out loud more to reassure myself than the dog.

It didn't take Harley long to find a spot that had most likely been marked by other dogs on numerous occasions. "If you behave, I'll get you something special when we get home." I didn't say the word "treat" because my dog was smart and knew what it meant.

There weren't any other pet owners waiting to see Jackson when I led Harley inside. A young woman with her dark hair braided down her back and wearing light purple scrubs looked up from her computer screen and smiled. "Good afternoon. How can I help you?"

I walked over to the counter. "I'm Brinley Brubaker, and I have an appointment for my dog Harley."

"Great," she said, glancing back at her screen. "It looks like we're doing a regular exam and shots today, correct?"

"Yes," I said.

"Why don't we start by getting his weight?" She came out from behind her desk and pointed toward the corner of the room at an industrial-style scale big enough to accommodate large dogs.

Getting Harley to stand on the smooth silver surface took a little coaxing. After quite a bit of wiggling, a little cooing, and some head scratching, he finally settled down enough for his weight to appear on the screen.

"If you'd like to follow me, we'll get you set up in an exam room," the woman said.

The drop-down table mounted to the wall had already been lowered. Nicely framed pictures with cute hand-painted kittens and puppies adorned one of the walls. During my initial online research into animal care shortly after adopting Harley, I'd learned that being in a new place with unfamiliar smells could be stressful for pets. I didn't want to risk him having an accident, so I sat in one of the chairs and pulled him into my lap. "You are being such a good boy," I murmured in his ear.

The room had two doors, and a gentle rap sounded on the one across from us. The door swung open, and Jackson peeked his head through the gap and said, "Brinley" before stepping inside.

After looking at the dark blue scrubs and how they enhanced the color of his eyes, I didn't doubt he could make any outfit look good. My appearance, on the other hand, was severely lacking. I hadn't had time to change before the appointment and still had on the shirt and shorts I'd worn to work.

"Hi," I said, getting to my feet. Harley whined and wriggled to get down, forcing me to adjust my hold.

Jackson set some syringes filled with liquid on the counter as he walked across the room. "Hey there, boy. Remember me?" Jackson held out his hand to Harley, palm up. "Why don't you put him on the table, and we'll take a look."

I complied and stayed close to reassure Harley that everything would be okay. I also wanted to know more about Jackson and said, "When we met at the pet boutique, you mentioned that you were fairly new to the area. How did you end up living here?"

"This was originally my grandfather's practice," Jackson said. "Before he decided to retire, he asked me to become his partner. He may tell everyone that he's retired, but the truth is, he still comes in a couple of times a month to see a few of his older customers."

Jackson opened my dog's mouth and checked his teeth. "How long have you had Harley?" he asked.

"Not long," I said. "He was a stray I found living near the beach."

"Do you know Archer Beckett?" I asked. "He owns The Flavored Bean coffee shop where I work."

"We've met," Jackson said, glancing up from running his hands along Harley's body. "He's a nice guy and one of my grandfather's friends."

"Anyway, he thinks Harley might have been abandoned."

"He's probably right," Jackson said, his tone somber. "It's more common than people think." He looked inside my dog's ears.

"I'm pretty good with faces, and I don't think Harley's ever been in to see us before."

That was a relief to hear. Now that I'd grown attached to the adorable critter, I would've been crushed to have to give him back to his owners.

"He looks good and healthy. I think the shots should be all he needs." Jackson grabbed the syringes and returned to the table. "How do you feel about ice cream?"

The question was a complete change of subject and caught me off guard. "Do you mean as in my favorite flavor or level of enjoyment?" I asked.

"Both." He chuckled and grinned.

"Chocolate fudge ripple, followed closely by mint chip," I said. "On a scale of one to ten, ice cream falls around nine."

"What scores a ten?"

I had to stop myself before I blurted out that he did. "Any dessert of the chocolate variety. The more decadent, the better."

"Compassionate and daring." He pinched the skin at Harley's nap and gave him his first shot. A shot that my dog didn't seem to notice. "Both qualities I admire."

I didn't need a mirror to know my cheeks were blazing a bright red. The heat skimming across my skin was all the sign I needed. "What about you? Since you're asking me about ice cream flavors, I assume you have a favorite." And a reason for wanting to know.

"Cotton candy...with extra sprinkles." He gave Harley his last shot.

"It takes a brave man to admit he likes a lot of sprinkles on his ice cream," I chided, glad to see that I wasn't the only one who could embarrass easily.

"And an even braver woman to be seen in public with a man and his excess sprinkles," Jackson said, then winked.

If I didn't know any better, his friendly banter had turned into a request for a date.

CHAPTER SEVENTEEN

I left Jackson's office elated that I had an ice cream date scheduled with the handsome vet for the following day.

By the time Harley and I got back to my aunt's house, Myrna and Vincent had arrived for game night. Only we'd already decided to forgo solving our weekly online mystery murder and focus on our real one.

The delicious aroma of something barbecued enticed Harley and me toward the kitchen, where I found everyone sitting at the table waiting for me. They'd ordered takeout and already had plates and utensils set out for the meal.

"How did it go at the vet's?" Delia asked as soon as I walked into the room. Harley spotted the food she'd put in his bowl and shot past me to reach it.

I giggled. "As you can see, Harley's doing great."

"And Jackson?" Myrna asked, wiggling her brows. "Is he doing great as well?"

Thankfully, Vincent didn't involve himself in their matchmaking efforts and gave the women one of his exasperated eye rolls on my behalf.

Delia tsked at him as she got out of her chair. After

opening the refrigerator door, she asked me, "Water, iced tea, or soda?"

"Water's fine," I said, taking my usual seat.

We spent the next twenty minutes enjoying the meal and catching up on trivial things, which included seeing all the new pictures Myrna had taken of Ziggy with her cell phone.

Once we'd finished cleaning up and were about to head to Delia's office, I asked the group, "Instead of staying here and going over everything we've uncovered, what do you say about taking Harley for a walk?" I needed time to work through the details about Myles's murder that were still bothering me. Sometimes a change of scenery helped clear my mind, making things easier to resolve.

"I think that's a great idea," Delia said, then joined Myrna in staring at Vincent as if he was going to find the idea appalling and argue.

"Stop glaring," Vincent grumbled. "I don't have a problem with getting some exercise and fresh air."

I snapped my pack around my hips and retrieved Harley's leash. "Hey, boy, what do you say about a stroll on the beach?" He wagged his tail and made a noise as if he understood me, then did a doggy dance around my feet. I leaned over, scratched his head, then attached the clip to the collar before following the group through the living room. Once outside, I gave Harley a stern look. "And no chasing Quincy, all right?"

The sun wouldn't set for a couple more hours, so we had plenty of time for a leisurely stroll. After leaving Delia's neighborhood, we stayed on the sidewalk and headed toward the Bean. Most of the time, I took Harley to the park, but I wanted to avoid running into people we knew from the retirement community.

A musical tune emanating from my hip startled me. I unzipped my pack, pulled out my cell phone, and saw Zoey's name on the screen. "Hey, Zoey," I answered. "What's up?"

"I'm calling about the covert mission you sent me on."
I envisioned her glancing around to see if anyone was
listening, then cupping her mouth while she talked.

"What did you find out?"

"I talked to three different people who were at Tori's
the day I picked up cheesecake," Zoey said. "One of them
couldn't remember where he'd heard about Myles's bad
business practices, but two of them were adamant that
they'd gotten the information from Natalie."

After the conversation Delia and I had with Claire, the
news wasn't surprising. "Thanks and good job. I'll let
everyone know." Zoey hadn't been talking loud, so I
wasn't sure if anyone standing close to me would be able
to overhear our conversation. Since the ones in question
were Myrna, Delia, and Vincent, who'd scooted closer to
eavesdrop, I asked, "Did you hear what Zoey said, or do
you need me to repeat it?" As soon as they stepped back, I
shared Zoey's information with them anyway.

"That puts a new perspective on things," Vincent said.

Before anyone could respond, Delia said, "It looks like
someone else had the same idea we did."

Besides Carson, I didn't think any other locals were
trying to solve Myles's murder, and I was confused by her
comment. "What do you mean?" I asked.

"Someone is sitting at our table," Delia said, pointing at
the shop's deck, which had been our intended destination.

"Can you tell who it is?" Myrna asked as she pushed
her glasses further up her nose and squinted.

"It looks like Archer's back," Vincent said, his gravelly
voice lacking some of his usual grumpiness. It was the
closest he ever came to expressing a positive emotion.

Everyone seemed to pick up their pace at the same
time, and it didn't take us long to reach the coffee shop.
"Hey, Archer," I said, stopping on the sidewalk to peer up
at him through the rails on the deck.

Archer had made himself comfortable and had his feet
propped on the edge of another chair. "Hey back. Why

don't you all come up and join me?" He balanced a bottle of beer on his lap and patted the cooler sitting beside his chair.

"Don't mind if I do," Vincent said, heading for the stairs with Myrna and Delia following behind him. Since Harley had yet to do his business, I unclipped his leash so he could run around the beach, then stayed below to keep an eye on him. "When did you get back?" I asked once everyone had settled around the table next to Archer.

"A few hours ago," he said.

I tried not to feel hurt that he hadn't bothered to respond to any of my messages. Our working relationship was still new. This was the first trip he'd taken and left me in charge, so I wasn't sure what to expect. Maybe not checking in was a norm for him. Intent on finding out, I asked, "Didn't you get my texts?"

"I'm afraid not," Archer said. "I would've called to check in, but my phone fell overboard while I was wrestling with a massive mackerel." He winked, so I didn't know if he was telling a fish tale, common among fishermen, or if he didn't want to tell us the real reason he'd lost his phone.

"Did you at least manage to save the fish?" Vincent asked, twisting the top off the bottle Archer had handed him.

"Of course," Archer said.

"If you couldn't reach us, weren't you worried that something might have happened to the place while you were gone?" I asked.

Archer glanced around and smiled. "The building's still standing, so you must have done a good job. I trust you, Brinley. So no, I wasn't worried." He gave his bottle a thoughtful tap. "If you were worried about reaching me, I take it something did happen." He took a long swallow of his drink. "Why don't you fill me in?"

I leaned against the railing. "Do you know Myles Mumford?"

"Yeah," Archer said. "He's an okay guy. Why do you ask?"

"Because his death wasn't an accident," Myrna blurted. "Brinley found his body on the beach."

"Leave it to you to get right to the point," Vincent said.

"What?" Myrna said. "There's no point in sugarcoating the obvious."

"I'm pretty sure it wasn't clear to Archer since he's been out of town," Delia said, trying to be supportive, yet act as a referee.

"I thought he fell off his boat." Archer straightened in his seat. "Are you saying he drifted ashore?"

"No, he was buried," I said. "At least partially when Harley found him."

"No wonder you wanted to get a hold of me," Archer said. "I take it there's also been some sleuthing going on in my absence."

"There has," I said, then proceeded to tell him everything from Landon having Carson interrogate Delia to all the tidbits of information we'd learned so far.

Archer drained the last of his beer. "It sounds like you've ruled out pretty much everyone except Natalie and Dean."

Myrna harrumphed. "I still think we should consider Ariel."

"Only because you don't like her," Delia said.

"Well, maybe, but there's still the cheating angle," Myrna said. "And you know what they say about jealous spouses."

"We do, but in this case, I'm leaning towards it being one of the Swaffords," I said. "Especially after learning that Natalie was the one who'd started the bad business dealing rumors about Myles."

"I agree," Delia said.

"Me too," Vincent said. "Now we need to figure out how to prove it."

Harley's bark had me spinning around and searching

for Quincy. I'd gotten so involved in the conversation that I hadn't paid much attention to him. The cat seemed to be getting bolder with each of their encounters. Quincy was rubbing up against the base of a palm tree, not bothering to hide his arrival from Harley.

The taunt was reciprocated with another bark and Harley kicking up sand as he chased after the cat. "Darn it, Harley. We talked about this," I groaned and took off after him, cringing when I heard the gang's laughter.

CHAPTER EIGHTEEN

As usual, the instant Harley barked, Quincy raced for the gap between the palm trees. A few seconds later, I lost sight of my dog as well.

The part of me that thought it wise to avoid what used to be the crime scene urged me to go around the trees and rocks to catch Harley. Too bad my curiosity acted like a mystery magnet and drew me to the spot.

The place where Harley and I'd found Myles showed no signs that his body had ever been there. Someone had filled in the hole and smoothed the sand.

At least when I stepped into the small clearing, I didn't find Harley digging or tugging on an arm that belonged to a dead person. Instead, he was prancing and whining at Quincy, who'd climbed up on a rock, the perfect place to remain out of reach so he could torment my dog the same way Luna did.

I used the temporary distraction to snag Harley and clip the leash to his collar. "Thanks, Quincy," I called after the cat as he jumped from the rock and disappeared into the tall grass. I was about to head back to the Bean when I heard mumbled voices coming from the same direction Quincy had gone.

Teenagers occasionally used the beach to make out,

and I didn't want to embarrass them by popping out into the open. I peeked around the clump of rocks Quincy had vacated to get a better look and was shocked to see Claire tromping through the sand, trying to keep up with Natalie. "What's Dean doing way out here?" she asked.

It didn't take much effort to deduce that Natalie had lured Claire out here with some fabricated story about Dean being hurt.

Had Natalie done the same thing with Myles? Had she told him Claire was in trouble to get him to come to the beach? If he cared anything at all for Claire, I could easily see it working. If she'd planned things ahead of time, had she arrived with a shovel, then smacked him over the head the instant he turned his back on her?

And if I was right, then Natalie was the one who'd murdered Myles to get him out of the way so Claire would get back together with her father. Only her plan hadn't worked. If our group of non-professional sleuthers had come close to figuring things out, then no doubt Carson was close or had already identified the killer and was gathering solid evidence to make an arrest.

If Natalie was as emotionally unbalanced as I thought, then what would she do to Claire for not complying with her wishes?

I huddled next to Harley, keeping us hidden in case the women changed direction. My concerns weren't necessary because a few seconds later it became clear that Natalie had a different place in mind. An area more scenic, farther along the beach, and potentially a lot more dangerous.

I'd watched the waves splash against the base of the rock formations from a distance during my walks with Harley, but I'd never ventured over to check them out. Drowning wasn't the main issue. Anyone unwise enough to climb near the edge risked slipping off and landing on the sharp rocks below. According to Zoey, there'd been a few injuries and at least one fatality over the years.

From where my friends were sitting, they couldn't see

this portion of the beach. They wouldn't have noticed the other women arrive. I didn't want to end up like Myles, but I was determined to help Claire. Since I couldn't predict how Natalie would react to my presence, handling the situation alone wasn't an option. I pulled out my cell and typed in the words, "Need help on the beach", selected the names of everyone in the group, then added Carson's and hit the send key.

After scooping Harley into my arms, I left my hiding spot and trailed after them. Running across the sand wasn't easy, not when I was carrying additional weight in the form of a squirming dog.

Harley wasn't happy about being jostled and dug the nails on his hind paws into my abdomen. I refused to put him down and didn't have time to worry about my discomfort, not when Claire's life could be in jeopardy.

They were almost to the edge of the rocks. I was afraid I wouldn't reach them in time, so I shouted their names as loud as I could.

Claire was the first to see me and stop.

"Brinley," Natalie said as she also slowed to a halt. She forced a smile, but not fast enough to disguise her irritated glare. "What are you doing out here?"

"Taking Harley for a walk," I said, continuing to move in their direction until I was a few feet away from them.

"I don't want to be rude, but we need to go. Dean could be in trouble," Claire said, the urgency in her voice bordering on panic.

If things went terribly wrong, I'd need my hands free to protect myself. I set Harley on the ground but kept the leash taut, so he remained near my feet and out of Natalie's reach. "Your father's not over there, is he, Natalie?" I asked.

Claire's expression changed from concern to confusion. She jerked her attention from me to Natalie. "What's she talking about?"

I turned to Claire. "Didn't you think it was strange that

Natalie brought you to the same stretch of beach where Myles died?"

"I, I guess I was too worried about Dean to give it much thought," Claire said.

"Personally, I thought it was poetic," Natalie stated smugly. She gave us her back and strode to a nearby boulder where she'd hidden a wooden paddle. Quite possibly the same object she'd used to murder Myles and had planned to use on Claire until I'd interceded.

"No." Claire sobbed as the pieces of what happened to the man she'd cared about clicked into place. "It was you?" she asked, her voice cracking in disbelief.

"I thought if Myles was out of the way, you and my dad...that things could be the way they were again," Natalie said.

Claire was past the point of being sympathetic and raised her voice at Natalie. "You can't control people's feelings or manipulate them into doing what you want."

Claire could've saved her breath. Natalie wasn't listening. Her eyes had a glazed-over quality as if her thoughts had drifted elsewhere and tuned out her surroundings.

The overwhelming urge to rush her now and wrestle the paddle away from her didn't last long. Natalie snapped out of her semi-trance and pinned me with an unsettling glare. "And you," she snarled, pointing the paddle in my direction. "Things would've worked out if you hadn't been snooping around on the beach and dug up Myles's body."

The storm had been responsible for uncovering Myles, not me. There was no way I'd be able to change Natalie's mind, so I didn't bother trying.

Natalie took a threatening step toward me, and my world turned into chaos.

CHAPTER NINETEEN

"Brinley!" Delia's frantic screech filled the air and distracted Natalie.

I glanced toward the sound of her voice and spotted Vincent, Archer, and Myrna sprinting alongside her.

As soon as they reached us, Myrna leaned forward, hands on her knees, and panted. She wouldn't be much help but deserved credit for coming to my aid anyway.

"What's the emergency?" Archer asked, his gaze going from me to Claire and Natalie.

I didn't get a chance to explain that I'd thwarted an attempt on Claire's life. The arrival of the makeshift cavalry must have jarred Claire from her frozen state. She screamed like a banshee and threw herself at Natalie. Once she had her pinned in the sand, Claire wrestled the paddle from her hand, then proceeded to pummel her body and yank her hair.

"Get off me," Natalie said, defensively blocking Claire's swings and attempting to get in a few of her own.

Vincent and Archer were finally able to pull Claire off, and when they did, clumps of Natalie's strands came away with Claire's fingers.

Rather than getting to her feet and running, Natalie

rolled on her stomach and crawled toward the paddle. I wasn't sure what she thought she'd accomplish. There were too many of us to fight off. All I knew was if she got her hands on the paddle and started swinging, one or more of us could sustain injuries before we disarmed her.

After snatching Harley off the ground and thrusting him safely into my aunt's arms, I dove for the paddle. I clutched it to my chest and rolled before Natalie could reach it. I sprang to my feet and waved it like a sword. "Don't even think about it," I said, refusing to let her sit up. I didn't think she could hurt anyone as long as she stayed sprawled on her back.

The glare Natalie leveled at me was filled with malevolence. I had no doubt if she wrestled the paddle away from me, she wouldn't hesitate to use it. I stepped back to avoid her reach but remained vigilant in my intimidation.

I could see the rest of the group from where I was standing. Harley was whining and struggling to get down. Delia was doing her best to keep him in her arms. Claire's burst of anger had dissipated. She had her head pressed against Vincent's shoulder, sobbing. His discomfort at dealing with an emotional woman was apparent in his rigid stance. He patted her back as if she was a foreign object he didn't know how to remove from his body.

Archer showed his support by moving closer to me. If Natalie decided to try something, I didn't doubt he'd jump in to help. He was also perceptive and must have figured out what they'd interrupted. "I take it Natalie's the one."

"Yeah," I said.

Myrna was still bent over, panting. "Carson's," she rasped, then managed another breath. "On his way."

No sooner had the information left her lips than the deputy came running from the direction of the beach's parking lot with Douglas doing his best to keep up with him.

Carson surveyed the scene, his gaze locking on the paddle in my hand. "Brinley, would you like to explain what's going on? I was afraid someone else had died when I got your text."

He had no idea how accurate that statement might have been if I hadn't had the foresight to send for reinforcements. "I'll explain," I said, handing him the paddle, then crossing my arms. "But only if you promise not to lecture me afterward."

Carson glanced around, no doubt hoping someone besides me would tell him what he wanted to know. Natalie definitely wasn't going to say anything. When no one answered, he gritted his teeth and said, "Fine."

"First off, I found the person who killed Myles," I said, directing my gaze at Natalie. My aunt and our friends deserved a lot of the credit, but with all the warnings Carson had given us recently, I thought it best not to mention their involvement.

"You don't know what you're talking about." Like most criminals, when cornered, Natalie resorted to denial. "And you can't prove anything."

"Maybe not, but I can," Carson said. "Douglas, why don't you handcuff the prisoner and take her back to the station."

"Gladly," Douglas said, grinning as if he'd been given an important covert operation. Being new to the force and constantly under scrutiny, I understood if it felt that way.

"And don't forget to remind her about her rights," Carson said. He placed his hand on my elbow and urged me away from the group.

"Remember the day at the marina when I mentioned the stolen outboard?" Carson asked.

"Yeah," I said, surprised that he was willing to share information.

"It turns out someone found it beached farther up the coast and called it in. I'm pretty sure that's how Natalie got around when she killed Myles."

That made sense and would be a good way to avoid being seen. "Do you think she also used the outboard to get back and forth from the marina?" She had access to the keys to Myles's boat. It wouldn't be hard to tow the small craft behind the larger one, then use it to reach the shore.

Carson swept his hand through his hair. "I don't doubt it, but I won't know until after I talk to her."

Provided she was willing to give him the same details she'd shared with Claire and me. "If it helps, she admitted that she'd taken Myles's life and planned to do the same to Claire," I said.

"I'll need to get your full statement," Carson said. "Can you come down to the station tomorrow?"

"It shouldn't be a problem." I glanced at the rest of my group, now huddled together, expectantly waiting to see what happened next. "What about the others?"

"I'll have Douglas follow up with each of them," Carson said. "It will be good practice for him."

Even though Carson was hard on his underling, I was glad to hear he was also looking out for him.

Shortly after that, Douglas had Natalie handcuffed and was escorting her back to his vehicle. Carson had arrived separately and offered to take Claire home on his way to speak with Dean. Telling the man what had happened with his daughter wasn't something Carson didn't think should be done over the phone.

Once they were gone, I turned to the group. "I don't know about you guys, but I'd like to go home now. I've had all the excitement I can handle for one day." Maybe even for the rest of the week. At least that's what I thought until my phone rang, and Jackson's name appeared on the screen.

The odds of a guy changing his mind about going out, especially when the date happened to be the first, was something I worried about when I answered his call.

"How's it going?" he asked in that deep charming voice I found so appealing.

I hesitated a moment before answering. You never knew how people would react when you told them you'd recently tangled with a killer. I could've told him I was okay and left it at that, but thanks to Delia's motherly support and influence, I'd developed a need to be truthful.

"Other than preventing a murder, not bad." Before I could tell Jackson everything that had transpired, Myrna, Vincent, Delia, and even Archer, had gathered around me to eavesdrop on our conversation. Glaring at each of them had no effect, so I finally relented. "Jackson, it appears I have an audience. Would you mind if I put the call on speaker?"

Rather than ending his call gallantly by making excuses, he chuckled. "Not at all."

I tapped a button, then held the phone out so everyone could hear.

Myrna moved her head, so she was inches away from the screen. "Hey, Jackson. I understand you're taking Brinley for ice cream tomorrow."

"Myrna," I snapped, afraid her matchmaking tendencies would lead to asking Jackson his intentions.

"That was the plan," Jackson said.

"After everything that's happened, I think she's in dire need of support today," Delia interjected. "We're gathering at my place. Why don't you join us?"

The only thing I desperately needed was relaxation and cuddling my dog. Although, I wasn't opposed to spending some time with Jackson.

"I thought she was kidding," Jackson said, his playful tone replaced with concern. "Are you saying the murder thing was real?"

"Which is why we think you should—" Jackson didn't give Myrna a chance to finish. "Be at your place within the hour."

CHAPTER TWENTY

I had enough time to shower, change clothes, and apply a light coat of makeup before Jackson arrived. As soon as the doorbell rang, Harley raced from my bedroom and down the stairs, no doubt reaching the front door before Delia.

"Jackson," my aunt's voice echoed from the foyer. "Come in."

By the time I reached the bottom step, he'd stacked two small Styrofoam containers and a large crayon-colored shopping bag on the floor by his feet.

"Hey, Brinley," Jackson said, taking a few steps away from the circle my aunt, Vincent, Myrna, and Archer had formed around him. "How are you doing?"

"I'm fine," I said. "You didn't need to bring anything." We'd eaten our last meal of the day before going on our earlier walk, so I was curious to see what was in the containers and the bag.

"He brought ice cream for all of us," Delia said as she slipped the bag on her wrist and took the top container from the stack, leaving the other for Archer to carry. With the possibility of food in his near future, Harley quickly lost interest in our new guest and trailed into the kitchen after my aunt.

So much for our first date. I tried to keep the disappointment out of my voice when I said, "You didn't need to do that."

"I know, but I wanted to." Jackson gave Vincent a look, which prompted the older man to loop his arm through Myrna's. "I think Delia could use our assistance," Vincent said.

Myrna tsked but didn't stop staring at Jackson and me. "Archer can help her if she needs it. The man runs a coffee shop, after all."

"I'm pretty sure she needs you to supervise." Vincent gave Myrna's arm a tug when she refused to budge.

"Oh, I get it," Myrna giggled. She gave me a thumbs up before letting Vincent lead her into the kitchen.

Unless I wanted to run back up the stairs, there was nowhere to hide from my recent bout of embarrassment. "Sorry about that," I said.

"Don't be," Jackson said, smiling. "I have an older sister back home who's done way worse." He took my hand. "My mother would smack me upside the head if I showed up at someone's home empty-handed, and ice cream seemed appropriate. It wasn't my way of getting out of our date...in case you were wondering. I was hoping you'd agree to have dinner with me tomorrow night instead," Jackson said.

The flutters in my stomach were back, and I couldn't be happier. "That depends," I said.

He raised a brow. "On what?"

"On whether or not I get to see you eat sprinkles," I teased.

"Dinner it is." Jackson's grin formed dimples.

"Come on," I said, taking him to join the others. They'd bypassed the kitchen and had everything, including bowls, spoons, and a package of cones Delia kept in the cupboard, spread out on the patio table.

The sun had already set, but I could see the stars in the

evening sky even after Delia turned on the deck lights.

Myrna had an empty bowl in her hand and was waving her spoon through the air. "I still think Landon should apologize to Delia for having Carson put her through an unnecessary interrogation."

None of us had been surprised that the sheriff hadn't shown up during Natalie's apprehension. I thought it was a smart move because I wouldn't put it past Myrna to let Landon know exactly what she thought of him.

"We all know that's not going to happen," Delia said. "Because then he'd have to admit the real reason he pointed me out as a suspect."

"Do I want to know what they're talking about?" Jackson whispered in my ear.

"Probably not," I said, grabbing two bowls and handing one to him.

My chest tightened when I saw the ice cream container labeled "Chocolate Fudge Ripple." I snatched it off the table before anyone could open it. "You remembered." I raised up on my toes and pressed a gentle kiss to Jackson's cheek. "Thank you."

Normally, I'd spend some time getting to know a guy before showing any kind of affection. After defusing a life-threatening situation, I didn't think anyone would mind. Least of all Jackson, who immediately wanted to know what would happen if he ran to the store for a pint of mint chip.

Once we were all settled in the chairs scattered around the table, I scooped some ice cream onto my spoon, then closed my eyes and let the cold sweetness melt on my tongue.

Jackson drew me from my reverie by asking, "Do you make a habit of confronting criminals?" He worked at making sure to get as many sprinkles as possible onto the spoon of his own ice cream for his next bite.

"Every chance I get," I said, grinning when his blue eyes widened. "Though, this was my first time off-line."

"Aww, the mystery game thing," he said.

"How did you know about that?"

"Delia and Myrna have mentioned it a few times," Jackson said. "I always thought it sounded like fun."

"You'll have to join us the next time we meet," Delia said.

"I'd like that, thanks," he said.

Archer was leaning against the railing, and after licking the drizzle off the side of his cone, he said, "Brinley, I've been meaning to chat with you about something."

"What would that be?" I asked.

"Zoey told me you had a floater while I was gone. Care to explain?"

I'd forgotten all about Herman. We'd only provided Archer with the sleuthing details about Myles's death, not how disposing of the fish after its unfortunate demise had been the start of our latest mystery adventure.

I grinned at him and said, "It's actually an interesting story. Why don't you take a seat?" I nodded at the empty chair next to me. "And I'll tell you all about it."

* * *

ABOUT THE AUTHOR

Nola Robertson grew up in the Midwest and eventually migrated to a rural town in New Mexico, where she lives with her husband and three cats, all with unique personalities and a lot of attitude.

Though she started her author career writing paranormal and sci-fi romance, it didn't take long for her love of solving mysteries to have her writing cozies. When she's not busy working on her next DIY project or reading, she's plotting her next mystery adventure.

Made in the USA
Las Vegas, NV
16 November 2022